UPSTAIRS DOWNSTAIRS
II
In My Lady's Chamber

Upstairs
Downstairs II

In My Lady's Chamber

By
JOHN HAWKESWORTH

NELSON DOUBLEDAY, Inc.
Garden City, New York

Published by
Dell Publishing Co., Inc.
1 Dag Hammarskjold Plaza
New York, New York 10017

First published in Great Britain in 1973
by Sphere Books Ltd.
Copyright © Sagitta Productions Ltd., 1972

This book is based on the television series of *Upstairs Downstairs*, produced by the author for London Weekend Television Limited and created by Sagitta Productions Limited in association with Jean Marsh and Eileen Atkins. Rex Firkin was the Executive Producer and Alfred Shaughnessy was Script Editor of the series. The author wishes to acknowledge the fact that in writing the book he has drawn largely on material from television scripts by the following writers:

Charlotte Bingham and Terence Brady, John Harrison, Jeremy Paul, Alfred Shaughnessy, Anthony Skene, Rosemary Ann Sisson, Fay Weldon, Peter Wildeblood.

This book is dedicated to them and to the actors, directors, technicians and all the other people who worked so hard to make the production such a happy one.

UPSTAIRS DOWNSTAIRS
II
In My Lady's Chamber

CHAPTER ONE

There was a sharp difference of opinion in the servants' hall of 165 Eaton Place over Miss Elizabeth's choice of Vienna for her honeymoon. 'Miss Elizabeth' was now Mrs Kirbridge, having married Mr Lawrence Kirbridge on a sunny June day in that same year of Our Lord nineteen hundred and eight, but the servants still found it very difficult to call her by her new name.

Rose, the head house parlourmaid, thought of Vienna as a romantic paradise. In her mind she could clearly see Miss Elizabeth twirling lightly through the woods in the arms of her beautiful new swain while a vast but hidden orchestra of violins played waltzes as the Danube swirled and splashed beyond them, deep blue in the moonlight. Mrs Bridges, the cook, didn't agree with her.

'I wouldn't want to spend *my* honeymoon among a lot of foreigners, I know that,' she said firmly, looking at Mr Hudson, the butler, who had once suggested himself as a future partner when their days in service were over. Mr Hudson nodded his agreement. He hated the Germans with a deep and bitter hate and as far as he was concerned Austria was tarred with the same Teutonic brush. If and when the time came for him to take Mrs Bridges as his lawful wedded wife his choice for a honeymoon would hover between Felixstowe and Paignton, it would certainly never be Vienna.

Lawrence Kirbridge found the Austrian capital almost as

delightful as Rose had imagined it; the wide leafy avenues, the great baroque palaces, the hundreds of gay street cafés and the flowers and the music inspired him to write poems and he felt quite drunk with pleasure. After a few days it all began to pall on Elizabeth. She felt rather sick as if she had eaten too much cream cake and the gaiety of the people took on a desperate quality and the bright lights and the gay façades seemed to be there only to cover up the decay beneath. One day they saw the Emperor Franz Josef at a military parade, bowed down under the weight of his decorations and his huge plumed helmet, like a very ancient walrus in fancy dress, he seemed to Elizabeth to typify his crumbling unwieldy country.

Elizabeth's feelings were prejudiced by another more personal worry. Lawrence was the most amusing and delightful companion anyone could wish for. He danced with his young bride, he serenaded her with poetry and told her how beautiful she was a hundred times a day. But that was all.

Although Elizabeth was twenty-three years old and had been allowed to lead a remarkably unfettered life for a girl of her class she had very little idea what exactly the physical act of making love entailed. Whispered conversations with her most intimate friends had only produced the wildest and most unlikely suggestions. There was general agreement that it was something that would be revealed with startling clarity on the marriage bed. It was also agreed that it was something definitely unpleasant and painful like a minor operation or going to the dentist and that all husbands became suddenly and inexplicably cruel and brutal when it came to this particular moment. Whatever happened it was the wife's solemn duty to submit and to bear her husband as many children as their parents thought fit; after that there was a possibility that in time making love could become a pleasure and even take place with other men if it was kept a dark secret and they were of the same class.

Lawrence was neither cruel nor brutal. For two nights he didn't even touch Elizabeth's body in the huge painted bed in Sacher's Hotel. On the second morning he asked her to take off her nightdress and she obeyed him with a feeling of fear and yet of increasing excitement. He gazed at her body for a long time in silence and then wrote a poem about her breasts. Elizabeth had no idea why the incident made her feel so unhappy but she believed that Lawrence realised the fact because that same evening, when he had drunk rather too much champagne, he told her that nothing must be allowed to spoil the perfection of their holiday but that back home in England when they were settled in their own house things would be different. Elizabeth had to be content with that.

The day her engagement was announced in *The Times,* Elizabeth and her mother, Lady Marjorie Bellamy, had begun the activity described by Lawrence as 'nest building'. As Lawrence was a poet there was no need to live in the middle of London, but neither of them particularly wanted to live in the depths of the country and the ugly red brick rash of new suburbs which was rapidly encircling the metropolis was to be avoided at all costs. It was Richard Bellamy, Elizabeth's father, who had the brain wave in suggesting Greenwich. He had come to know the district quite well when he was Under Secretary at the Admiralty in the previous Tory Government. Elizabeth and Lawrence were immediately attracted to the place which had the charm of a Georgian

3

village but was within easy travelling distance of London. A local agent produced a pleasant terraced house in a quiet square for the annual rent of one hundred pounds, including rates and taxes.

Elizabeth was overjoyed when her mother offered her the loan of Rose until the new establishment was running smoothly. Rose had been her friend and confidante ever since she could remember and Elizabeth's personal maid since she had become a young lady four years before. Mr Hudson took the temporary loss of his head house parlourmaid philosophically; in a remote but satisfactory sort of way Rose's presence at Greenwich would extend his own authority.

'Mrs Kirbridge not being experienced as a lady of the house,' he counselled Rose before she left, 'it will be up to you to maintain standards in the kitchen and elsewhere.'

'I don't know so much about the kitchen,' said Mrs Bridges on behalf of all culinary establishments everywhere, 'there'll be a cook in charge of the kitchen, Mr Hudson.'

Mr Hudson realised that his diplomacy had been at fault.

'Very true, Mrs Bridges,' he replied. 'But a cook-general is not quite the same as . . . well . . . as what we have here.'

Mrs Bridges responded to his blandishments with a satisfied smile.

'I am not suggesting that Rose should usurp the cook's authority in the kitchen,' the butler explained, 'but as far as serving and dishing up and running the household, Rose will have big responsibilities, and I want to make sure she takes them seriously.'

He faced Rose directly.

'Remember, my girl, that you will be there as a representative of the Bellamy household.'

4

'Oh yes I will, Mr Hudson,' Rose assured him in a dedicated tone of voice.

Upstairs in the morning room the conversation was also touching on the new cook at Greenwich. Lady Marjorie had engaged a woman called Mrs Fellowes who seemed both clean and adequately capable.

'I agreed to pay her thirty pounds a year,' Lady Marjorie told Elizabeth and Lawrence. 'I hope that is all right?'

The young couple had neither of them the faintest idea of the current wages received by cook-generals on the outskirts of London.

'I'm sure it is,' Elizabeth answered dutifully.

'Then with Rose you'll only need a daily help and perhaps a jobbing gardener,' Lady Marjorie went on, thinking the matter settled.

'Oh, and Lawrence's manservant,' said Elizabeth.

Lady Marjorie assumed a blank expression which showed she was put out. She had not approved of her only daughter marrying a penniless poet whose only assets seemed to be that he was a gentleman and had pleasant manners; now she suspected that he was beginning to take advantage of his favoured position.

'I'm afraid I didn't know about that,' she said with a bewildered shrug.

'Oh it's quite all right,' Lawrence explained blandly. 'I advertised for one before we left. I put my mother's address for replies—I didn't want to bother you.'

Lady Marjorie's suspicions of a plot appeared well founded.

'You would have to pay a man fifty pounds a year; do you

really think you can afford it?' she said, looking at her daughter enquiringly. After all it was all her money they were talking about.

'Perhaps a bootboy,' Lady Marjorie suggested helpfully.

'Oh no, I must have a manservant! Such a delightful expression—"a manservant",' Lawrence replied. 'Gives one something to live up to. Sets one's standards.'

'Well if you think you can manage,' Lady Marjorie retorted, as gloomily as possible.

'Lawrence hopes to write some articles and he'll be paid for those and the *Pall Mall* has asked him for two reviews already and then there's the book of poems.' Elizabeth catalogued her husband's current achievements.

'That's excellent,' said Lady Marjorie coldly. 'I suppose it's the same with everything in life—you start in a small way and work your way up.'

She wasn't going to let them get swollen headed over a couple of reviews and a book of poems.

'Except that a poet isn't *quite* like a draper's assistant,' Lawrence explained in a dry voice, 'moving on through socks and ties to silk handkerchiefs.'

Lady Marjorie looked up sharply. It was the first time Lawrence Kirbridge had been positively rude to her.

Later on when Lawrence had gone off to see his publisher Lady Marjorie counselled her daughter about the problems of money and the matrimonial state.

'When I married your father, darling,' she told Elizabeth, 'he wasn't a rich man.'

'He isn't now, is he?' said Elizabeth.

'No. But what is mine is his, naturally,' Lady Marjorie

went on, thinking her daughter was being rather deliberately obtuse. 'What I mean is that it isn't easy for a man to marry a wife whose family has more money than he has.'

'Oh mother!' Elizabeth answered impatiently. 'We don't care about that! Money isn't as important to us as it is to you.'

'Money is always important if you haven't enough of it,' Lady Marjorie replied. She knew the remark was not original but she believed it to be true. 'Let Lawrence make the decisions,' she added. 'Your marriage will never succeed if you don't.'

'But it will if I do?'

Lady Marjorie shook her head sadly; it was extraordinary the way Elizabeth always seemed to delight in twisting round the simplest statement.

The day they moved to Greenwich Rose saw a strange young man standing in the area peering in at the windows of the kitchen. She pointed him out to Elizabeth who was about to open the front door.

The man looked up at them and raised his bowler hat.

'Good afternoon,' he called up at them. 'I've come to see Mr Kirbridge,' and began to ascend the area steps.

'I don't like his face,' Rose hissed in Elizabeth's ear. 'He looks like a debt collector.'

The young man produced a letter from Lawrence promising him an interview for the post of valet.

'My husband isn't back yet,' Elizabeth explained, secretly cursing Lawrence for being away and landing her with this extra problem. 'Perhaps you could come back another day.'

The man stood his ground. He was tall and dark and Welsh, decidedly Welsh.

'I've come a long way, madam,' he said very quietly. It wasn't exactly a threat but it was firmly spoken.

'Well I'll see you myself then,' Elizabeth decided and opened the door.

The man helped the cab driver and Rose to carry in the luggage. He smiled at Rose as they bumped cases and Rose responded with an icy, disdainful stare.

Elizabeth was pleased with the drawing room. It was small but it was light and pleasant and uncluttered. She was opening the doors that divided it from the dining room when a voice made her start.

'You did say you'd see me now, madam.'

It was the man, humble and respectful, but still firm. Turning round Elizabeth saw that he was clasping his hat to his bosom as if he was about to break into a rendering of 'My Love is Like a Red Red Rose'. She almost giggled.

Looking back on the interview she came to the conclusion that it was Thomas Watkins who had interviewed her, not the other way round. Mr Watkins presented his credentials in the shape of impeccable references from a lady and gentleman in Llandudno. Elizabeth remembered something her mother had told her.

'Why did you leave your last employer?' she asked.

Mr Watkins smiled easily. 'They were going to Australia, madam.'

'Oh. Didn't you want to go with them?'

'No. Not enough scope out there from what I hear.'

Rose came into the room with the excuse that she needed the keys of the big trunk. As she left she made a face at

Elizabeth behind Mr Watkins' back indicating her disapproval of him.

'Well, I don't know there'll be a great deal of scope here,' Elizabeth replied, twisting the letter from the lady from Llandudno nervously in her fingers.

Mr Watkins didn't seem to agree with her.

'What would my duties be?' he asked.

Elizabeth hadn't the least idea. She tried to remember what Edward, the footman, did at Eaton Place.

'Duties?' she replied. 'Well, to look after the master's clothing, I suppose, and light the fire in the dressing room and keep it tidy.'

She was beginning to run out of ideas already.

'Oh and clean the boots,' she went on with sudden inspiration, 'and fill the coal scuttles and . . .'

'Clean the boots?' Mr Watkins queried in a way that made Elizabeth wonder if she had gone too far.

'If . . . if you wouldn't mind,' she almost pleaded.

'So I'd be a footman-valet.'

'Yes, that's right,' said Elizabeth with relief. 'We'd like you to wait at table and help out generally.'

Rose came in again, this time pretending the coal scuttle was empty which it wasn't.

'Indoors that is,' Elizabeth went on, ignoring Rose's look of annoyance. 'We thought we'd get a jobbing gardener.'

'Oh I don't mind seeing to the garden,' Mr Watkins replied, giving Rose a friendly little nod as she went out again.

'What would the wages be?' he asked suddenly, throwing Elizabeth off her balance again.

'Oh,' she tried to remember what her mother had said. 'Oh yes. Fifty pounds.'

Mr Watkins didn't show any emotion. Elizabeth waited anxiously.

'Fifty pounds—and a suit of clothes,' she added generously.

'Livery?' he asked suspiciously.

'I don't want you in livery. I think a black suit would be appropriate.'

This seemed to please the Welshman.

'Right you are, madam,' he said cheerily. 'I'll be along in the morning.'

Elizabeth turned away with a sudden awful thought. Supposing Lawrence didn't approve of Mr Thomas Watkins?

'Er . . . perhaps it would be better . . .' she looked up as the front door shut. He had gone and Rose was in his place.

'Excuse me, madam,' she said very coolly. 'Have you engaged that man?'

Elizabeth felt dazed.

'I suppose I have, Rose,' she admitted.

Rose didn't answer, she just sighed and shook her head.

'Cook wants to see you, madam,' she said.

'What's she like, Rose?'

'I'm sure I don't know,' Rose replied unhelpfully. But she did know and it partly accounted for her bad mood. Mrs Fellowes was a moaner. Already in the space of ten minutes she had twice complained about her bad leg and made it abundantly clear that under no circumstances could she be expected to lift anything heavy.

Thomas, as Mr Watkins came to be called, was an immediate success with Lawrence Kirbridge; he was an attentive and efficient manservant and had a pleasant turn of phrase which pleased the poet.

'Do you like being a valet?' Lawrence asked him one morning as Thomas was packing a suitcase for a weekend visit.

'I've no objection to it,' Thomas replied.

'I should have thought it would be rather a dead-end job,' Lawrence suggested.

'I wouldn't say that, sir,' Thomas replied carefully.

'Not many valets become Prime Minister,' said Lawrence as he tied his stock.

'Not many poets do, either,' the valet replied, quickly adding, 'Did you wish to take these socks with you, sir?'

Lawrence nodded.

'Every job's got scope, if you can find it,' Thomas went on, turning back to the suitcase.

'What scope can you find in being a valet?' Lawrence asked. Thomas straightened up.

'Well,' he said. 'Let's see, sir. You might become famous and travel all over the world reading your poems. I'd travel with you and perhaps I might meet some rich American lady—there's a lot of them about I believe—widows and so on—and I'd marry her.'

Lawrence smiled; the idea appealed to him.

'Or perhaps we might go to South Africa and I'd play cards with a man who couldn't pay me, but he'd give me a worthless scrap of paper instead which turns out to be a diamond mine. So there you are,' Thomas went on, scooping up Lawrence's hairbrushes and putting them in their case. 'I'd be a millionaire again. There's always scope somewhere.'

'Meanwhile you press my clothes.'

'Oh well, sir,' Thomas answered. 'You have to do a good job on whatever you're doing at the moment. You have to or you can't take advantage of the scope when you find it.'

To Elizabeth's delight and surprise, Rose soon changed her opinion about Thomas. She found he was willing and helpful and hard working. Together they conspired to laugh at or ignore Mrs Fellowes' endless complaints.

'I believe in making the best of life,' Thomas told Rose one evening as he was cleaning her boots. 'After all we're all in it together.'

'Well I suppose we are,' Rose replied.

'So we might as well enjoy it.' He lowered her leg to the floor.

'Come on, give us the other one then.'

Rose meekly put her other foot into Thomas' lap.

'You shouldn't be doing that, Thomas,' she said. 'It's not your place.'

Thomas laughed. 'I don't believe in people having places,' he said.

Rose was shocked.

'Don't you ever let Mr Hudson hear you saying that,' she warned him.

'Who's Mr Hudson when he's at home?' he asked.

'He's our butler at Eaton Place. A real proper butler.'

'Is he?' Thomas sounded unimpressed. 'What's it like at Eaton Place?'

Rose told him all about Eaton Place and its mysterious ways, making it sound almost as grand as Buckingham Palace.

'But it's nice there,' she said, not wanting to give Thomas a wrong impression. 'What I call friendly but dignified.'

'Dignified,' made Thomas smile.

'We're all friends down below stairs,' she explained. 'But we know where we are.'

'You mean you have to know your place,' he teased her.

'Yes. It wouldn't do for you, Thomas Watkins.'

He gave her boot a final polish.

'I don't know,' he said. 'I think I might like it. There's money there . . . bit of scope.'

'You've got a neat foot, do you know that, Rose,' Thomas told her as he lowered her leg to the floor. Rose flounced away pretending to be very put out at such a personal remark but a flush came to her cheeks. It was the first time anyone had flirted with her for a very long time.

A few days later Thomas was given the opportunity to see Eaton Place for himself. Elizabeth sent him there to collect two boxes of wedding presents that she had left behind.

'You will be careful, at Eaton Place, I mean, won't you!' Rose counselled him as he was leaving. 'I mean careful how you speak to Mr Hudson.'

'He's only a butler, isn't he?' Thomas replied loftily and watched Rose's horrified expression with delight.

Mr Hudson took an immediate dislike to Thomas Watkins, finding him a typical, sly, insolent, smooth-tongued example of a race he put at only one step better than foreigners. Their dislike was completely mutual. Apart from the butler, all else at Eaton Place found favour in Thomas Watkins' eyes. He liked the largeness and warmth of the place and the shiny big Renault car in the garage mews at the back and the richness of Mrs Bridges' walnut cake. Mrs Bridges liked Thomas Watkins for praising her walnut cake and asked him to come and join her in the kitchen for a quiet cup of tea and a gossip, an honour bestowed on very few.

'Fancy him staying away for a whole weekend without

13

his wife,' Mrs Bridges exclaimed when Thomas had let slip that particular piece of domestic news. 'It doesn't seem right, not with a newly wedded couple in their love nest so to speak; still, I don't expect Mr Kirbridge is used to living in a household yet.'

Mrs Bridges was always prepared to give the benefit of the doubt. 'A bachelor gets accustomed to coming and going as he pleases, with meals at all hours,' she explained.

'He does that all right,' said Thomas, taking another bite of cake.

'Does what?' Mrs Bridges demanded, all agog.

'It's being a poet, I suppose,' Thomas went on with his mouth rather full. 'He must have got in the way of working by himself at night.'

He looked round carefully in a conspiratorial sort of way and lowered his voice.

'Sometimes he sleeps in his dressing room,' he confided to the cook. Mrs Bridges was shaken; she didn't like the sound of it. Not at all.

CHAPTER TWO

Lawrence Kirbridge was the only child of elderly parents. His father had died when he was only seven years old and the consequence was that his mother had spoilt him remorselessly. At public school he had turned into a goodlooking boy, brilliant rather than clever, and inclined to be lazy. At Oxford and later in London as a young man his physical beauty and witty tongue had made him friends wherever he chose to look. It was Lawrence's misfortune that success came so easily for him and put him off his guard so that when an evil genius came into his life he was unable to resist her. She came in the shape of a Birmingham school teacher's daughter called Evelyn Larkin, the leader of a quasi-artistic political group with extreme ideas into which Lawrence had unexpectedly drifted. Evelyn was a ruthless predator more interested in Lawrence's body than his mind. She took him as her slave and used him for her pleasure, leaving him disgusted and humiliated and afraid. Confronted with a young wife with a beautiful body only too obviously willing and needing him to make love to her he felt no desire for her, only the fear of a humiliating disaster.

He had known all this long before he became engaged to Elizabeth; but whenever anything unpleasant turned up in his life Lawrence had developed a trick of putting it aside and running away from it as even now he was for ever running away to London or to stay with friends for the weekend;

staying up at night pretending to work until Elizabeth was asleep, inventing any excuse to keep out of the way, avoiding and yet dreading the day he would have to face up to reality.

As the weeks went by Elizabeth began to feel ill and to cry and to lose her temper at the least silly thing. She was lonely, unhappy and unloved and she didn't understand why and her husband was unable to tell her. Rose on the other hand was blooming in the warmth of Thomas Watkins' attentions.

One afternoon she was taking a vase of dead flowers downstairs and humming happily to herself when Elizabeth heard her and it annoyed her intensely. She went in to Lawrence who was in the drawing room reading in the paper the startling news that a quarter of the surviving veterans of the Crimean War were in the workhouse.

'Did you hear that, Lawrence, Rose humming again; it really is most irritating. I must talk to her about it,' she said. 'I don't know what's come over her.'

Lawrence looked up. 'Could it be,' he suggested, 'that the desires of the virginal nymph, Rose, are aroused by the dark masculinity of the Welsh bull?'

Elizabeth turned on him.

'I find that remark cheap and disgusting.'

Lawrence stood up and shut his paper and went out.

'Nearly time for my train,' he said at the door. He was off to read some poems to a group at Cambridge.

That evening after supper Elizabeth found she couldn't concentrate on sewing or reading or anything at all so she decided to go to bed early. As she reached the bottom of the stair she heard muffled laughter from the kitchen and something like a squeal from Rose. She went down the stairs to the basement. Thomas was chasing Rose round the kitchen. As she stood watching Thomas caught Rose who pretended unsuccessfully to resist his kiss. Something in Elizabeth exploded.

'How dare you!' she shouted and the servants drew apart, guilty and surprised. 'How dare you behave like that!' Elizabeth continued, her voice growing increasingly hysterical. 'It's absolutely disgusting! I won't have it in my kitchen. I won't! You can both take a week's notice. Both of you,' she added, glaring at Rose and then turned and ran up the stairs to her room and threw herself on her bed.

After ten minutes Rose crept up the stairs to the landing where she could hear Elizabeth weeping in her room. She went in quietly and took Elizabeth in her arms and comforted her as she had done so many times in the past.

The next morning Elizabeth had breakfast in bed and then rang for Rose to come up and dress her. There was still a noticeable uneasiness between them.

Rose suggested the cream day dress, but Elizabeth insisted on the new pink one with the sash.

'Are you going out then, madam?' Rose asked.

'No,' Elizabeth replied, examining her face gloomily in the dressing table mirror. 'I just feel like dressing up. It might make me feel as if I had something to do . . .'

Rose stood still and pursed her lips.

'Madam. Thomas and I would like to apologise for . . . for what happened last night. It won't occur again.'

Elizabeth looked round at her.

'I see. All right, Rose.' She was rather taken by surprise by the apology.

'Do you love Thomas, Rose?'

It was Rose's turn to be taken by surprise.

'Well Miss Lizzie. I really don't know,' she said in confusion.

'I hope you're not being very silly,' Elizabeth went on. 'Letting him take advantage of you.'

'Oh Miss Lizzie,' Rose exclaimed. 'It was only in fun. I wouldn't put up with anything that wasn't proper before I was married. You should know that.'

'Oh,' Elizabeth answered. 'You haven't ever . . . he hasn't . . . ?'

'Never!' Rose was shocked. 'Of course not! What are you thinking of, Miss Lizzie?'

'Oh I don't know.' Elizabeth put her hands up to her temples in an almost desperate gesture. 'I thought you might be able to help me, that's all.'

Rose began to comb Elizabeth's hair which always had a way of making her feel calmer.

'Don't you think men are difficult to understand?' she asked Rose after a while. 'Oh not fathers and brothers, but men. Just men.'

'I'm sure I don't know, Miss Lizzie,' Rose replied guardedly. 'Gentlemen are different from servants.'

'Don't you believe it, Rose.'

'Well, it stands to reason,' Rose went on. 'Men what haven't been properly educated just want one thing, that's what my auntie used to say, and we women have to suffer for it.'

Elizabeth looked at Rose in the mirror.

'Do you think it would be such suffering, Rose?' she asked.

'Well, I'm not a married woman am I? So how should I

know?' Rose was embarrassed. 'Why don't you ask your mother?'

'Unfortunately such things are not thought a proper subject of conversation between a mother and a daughter.'

Elizabeth stood up and allowed Rose to dress her.

'That's why I'm asking you.'

'Well my uncle was *brutal*, that's what my auntie used to say,' Rose answered, 'especially when he'd had a drop.'

Elizabeth wrinkled her forehead.

'I don't think that will ever be Mr Kirbridge's problem,' she said drily.

'Oh I didn't mean . . .' Rose exclaimed in horror. 'What have you got me saying, Miss Lizzie? We shouldn't be talking of such things.'

'Nobody ever seems to talk of such things,' Elizabeth answered.

'Well I've got a pile of ironing to do in the kitchen,' Rose said firmly, and began to retreat.

'And Thomas will be there . . . and he'll tease you, and make you laugh.'

'And nothing, Miss Elizabeth. I've got my work to do and so has he.'

Elizabeth sighed deeply.

'And it would all be so easy, so easy,' she murmured to herself.

The next evening Lawrence came to bed as usual very late. Elizabeth hardly slept at all and her worries and unhappiness took on gigantic nightmarish shapes. Early in the morning she determined that she must swallow her pride and talk frankly to Lawrence.

When he moved to get up she held his arm.

'Lawrence,' she begged, 'when . . . ?'

It wasn't exactly what she had planned to say. Lawrence shrugged. 'When?' he said blankly.

'Oh darling, you know what I mean,' Elizabeth pleaded. As he couldn't escape, he became evasive.

'We . . . we aren't really settled yet,' he said.

'About as settled as we ever shall be,' Elizabeth replied sadly.

'I'm sure it shouldn't . . .' he began uncertainly.

'What? What shouldn't what?' she answered sharply.

'Well . . . shouldn't worry you so much,' he replied with an unhappy shrug.

'We're husband and wife for Heaven's sake. At least everyone thinks we are.'

'Perhaps we should have stayed two people.' Lawrence sat on the bed.

'Two children I'm afraid you mean, Lawrence.'

He wasn't going to be drawn into the usual row.

'I wish,' he began, then he took her hands and kissed them, 'I love you, Elizabeth. Holding your precious hands . . . and reciting poetry between kisses. I love you so chastely, so tenderly. I couldn't bear to submit to anything crude. For me it is bliss enough . . .'

He touched her breast and Elizabeth shivered and drew away sobbing.

Elizabeth was already in the dining room when her husband came in. Her hair was untidy and her eyes red and she was in her dressing gown.

Lawrence didn't comment; in fact neither of them spoke until Rose left the room.

'Are you going out?' Elizabeth asked.

'Yes. Sir Edwin wants to see me about my book. The proofs are ready,' Lawrence answered and began eating. Lawrence's publisher was called Sir Edwin Partridge.

'When am I going to have the pleasure of meeting the famous Sir Edwin?' Elizabeth continued.

'Possibly next week,' Lawrence answered between mouthfuls, his eyes on the newspaper. 'I'm giving a little soirée to . . . to herald the publication. My first book after all.'

'I'll talk to Mrs Fellowes about it.'

'I've already spoken to Thomas,' Lawrence told her.

Elizabeth gazed at him in fury. It was her house and her money that would pay for his party.

'Thank you,' she said sweetly. 'Thank you very much. When will you be requiring me again?'

Lawrence looked up.

'Perhaps I put it wrongly,' she continued. 'Will you be requiring me again?'

'Please don't be childish, Elizabeth.'

'No, of course not. We must be very grown up people, mustn't we? Have you any idea why we got married?' she asked furiously.

Lawrence looked at his watch. 'This is a bad moment to examine our consciences. I have a train to catch.'

She wasn't going to let him run away again.

'It's always a bad moment with you,' she said, continuing with the attack. 'At night you're too busy writing. In the morning you're hurrying up to London. Every weekend you seem to go off without me, staying with people. Could I have an appointment perhaps?'

Lawrence looked at her.

'I wish you'd dress for breakfast,' he said.

'Is that the best you can do?' Elizabeth's voice was rising.

'If you wish to behave like a . . .' he began.

'Go on. Say it. Say it,' Elizabeth shouted. 'No, Lawrence. I'd much rather behave like a wife and a mother.'

'Elizabeth. Not at breakfast.'

He slammed his napkin down and made for the door but Elizabeth cut him off.

'You won't talk about it in bed.' She threw the words in his face.

It was a small house and Rose was uncomfortably aware of the angry words coming from the dining room as she helped Mrs Fellowes wash up. At last the front door slammed and there was silence.

'Cloud's burst up there all right,' said Thomas, coming down the backstairs into the kitchen and blowing the air from his cheeks.

'What were they saying then?' Mrs Fellowes wanted to know.

'Silence, Elizabeth!' said Thomas, imitating his master. 'That was him, like my old dad on a Saturday; and she yelling back at him like a Barry fishwife, calling him a common coal heaver.'

'Well I never,' said Mrs Fellowes gratified. 'Can you imagine Mr Kirbridge heaving coal?'

Rose's lips were pursed. 'And what was you doing?' she asked Thomas nastily, 'just standing there listening?'

'What else did they say?' asked Mrs Fellowes.

' "You're ill, Elizabeth," he says to her,' Thomas went on, pleased to have an appreciative audience. ' "And you Lawrence," she screams back at him, "is there nothing wrong with you?" Then she bursts into tears and runs upstairs nearly knocking me over on the way.'

Mrs Fellowes' mouth fell open at the thought and the bedroom bell began to jangle on the board.

'Civilised' was an adjective Sir Edwin Partridge would favour to describe himself. In middle-age he was a comfortable well-preserved bachelor able to indulge an experienced appetite for all things he considered beautiful. His office was furnished with a flamboyant masculine excellence that exactly reflected his personality—the private room of a connoisseur of elegance.

Years of experience had taught Sir Edwin a great deal about the inner workings of the talented young men whose poems he published successfully; even before Lawrence came into the room, the latest batch of poems had made him suspect that a note of discord had crept into the poet's life. Now he studied Lawrence's face as he glanced at the proofs, he could see clear signs of strain.

Sir Edwin bided his time.

'You haven't included any of the latest ones I notice,' Lawrence said at last.

'No,' Sir Edwin answered carefully. 'There are some things I don't understand.'

He took up a manuscript poem from the pile in front of him on the desk.

'This curiosity for instance. "Venus Arising from a Zinc Tub". Very Degas, my dear, but I don't think the public is quite ready for this sort of thing.'

Sir Edwin put on his spectacles and read from the page:

' "Bright Botticelli never saw such vegetable stew" '—he

quoted. 'That's unkind, Lawrence: Venus arising from her bath is *not* a vegetable stew.'

'I meant the flesh all overcooked,' Lawrence explained. Sir Edwin nodded. 'Sad stuff, my dear, for a young man just back from his honeymoon.'

He put down the manuscript.

'A young man with, so they tell me, a ravishingly beautiful young wife can do without such bilious thoughts.'

'I must write as I feel,' Lawrence answered. 'Am I to correct these?' He indicated the proofs in his hand.

'Naturally,' Sir Edwin replied. 'Take them home and share the pleasure with your proud lady.'

Lawrence stood up, evidently ill at ease, and Sir Edwin watched him closely.

'I wonder,' Lawrence said tentatively, 'could I . . . could I do it here? I promise not to disturb . . .'

Sir Edwin went over to him. 'I dare say we can find you a corner,' he said and put his arm round Lawrence's shoulder in a friendly way.

'Is there something troubling you, Lawrence?' he asked quietly. 'I'm unofficial godfather to all my protégés. Sometimes a few words with an older man can help.' He made a gesture with his free hand.

'I wouldn't wish to burden you, Sir Edwin,' Lawrence replied, confirming Sir Edwin's suspicions.

'But that's one of my functions,' the publisher went on smoothly. 'Burden bearer to the Muse.'

'I think perhaps I'm not the sort of man who should ever have married,' Lawrence confessed with difficulty.

Sir Edwin nodded and murmured a quiet understanding 'Ah.'

'I like Elizabeth very much. Which only makes me feel more of a cad.'

Sir Edwin refilled their glasses. 'Let's have a jaw about it,' he suggested and beckoned Lawrence to sit with him on the big leather sofa.

'I suppose one is too poetical about life altogether. Unfortunately. Well it was to do with something that happened in the past but . . . well anything . . . practical . . disgusts me.'

Sir Edwin nodded.

'So the honeymoon was a bit of a shock to . . . to both of you?' he probed gently.

'More or less,' Lawrence replied.

'Honeymoons are the invention of the Devil,' said Sir Edwin. 'I've always said so. If you love each other you may reach a modus vivendi in time.' He was probing again.

Lawrence shook his head. 'I don't think so. Elizabeth has —well, a very physical nature. I don't think she will ever be happy with a platonic arrangement.'

'Oh,' said Sir Edwin.

'As a matter of fact,' Lawrence went on, 'I'm afraid it may be making her ill.'

'You have . . . er . . . talked about it?' the publisher asked.

Lawrence nodded. 'A little,' he confessed.

'Brave,' said Sir Edwin and stood up.

'What can I do?' Lawrence begged of him.

'For the moment nothing. And certainly nothing that disgusts you; that will only succeed in disgusting her and we will have two sad youngsters on our hands. It would be a thousand pities if she were to sacrifice a warm nature.'

Sir Edwin made a plaintive gesture with his hands.

'Much as I feel for you, my dear boy, I am torn for both of you.'

'I've no wish to keep her from her . . . I suppose, her needs . . .' Lawrence struggled on, 'but . . .'

'But you cannot see her in that light,' Sir Edwin suggested lightly.

'Exactly. I love and respect her too much.'

There was a little silence which grew with the seconds until it seemed tangible like the cloud of smoke coming from Sir Edwin's cigar.

'Well,' said Sir Edwin, completely at a loss for once.

'You have befriended me . . .' said Lawrence.

Sir Edwin looked at him across the desk.

'Perhaps . . .' Lawrence continued, 'you would . . .'

'Befriend her?' Sir Edwin suggested.

Lawrence nodded.

'Very sticky,' Thomas whispered to Rose as he passed her handing round the champagne. Little groups of poets stood eyeing little groups of literary critics uneasily. No one seemed to know each other very well. Lawrence was beginning to feel that the whole evening was going to be a desperate failure. Then Sir Edwin arrived and all seemed changed in the twinkling of an eye. A wave of his gloved hand, a compliment or a joke as he made his triumphant progress round the room and suddenly everyone was talking and drinking happily together.

'It was so very kind of you to come, Sir Edwin,' Elizabeth assured him when they were introduced.

'Edwin please, if you can bear it,' Sir Edwin begged her. 'I think the reason most children howl at their christening is

because they can't bear the names they are given, don't you?'
He gave his hostess a look of evident admiration.

'. . . Although I should be surprised if you misbehaved at yours,' Sir Edwin continued. 'Elizabeth suits you perfectly.'

'Thank you,' Elizabeth answered, somewhat bewildered by the flow of words.

'And please don't think I'm one of those boring men who can't meet a woman without paying a compliment. I'm the plain dealer to my very soul,' Sir Edwin confessed, 'and when I say that Lawrence is the most exciting young poet since Bridges and his wife a vision of loveliness you must understand I am being no more than crudely factual.'

Overhearing these words a young critic from *The Poetry Review* hastily scribbled 'Bridges' on his cuff. 'What do you think of Kirbridge's poetry?' he asked the celebrated Tompkins of the *Morning Post*. 'Very little. Too gloomy. Negative. Won't do,' the great man replied.

'Quite a nice swing to it,' the *Poetry Review* man suggested.

'So has the hangman's rope,' said Tompkins, and took another glass of champagne from the tray offered to him by Rose.

No one present could say that the description 'a vision of loveliness' was not a fair description of Elizabeth Kirbridge. For Lawrence's sake she had taken a great deal of trouble with her appearance. She wore a white dress which well displayed her tiny waist and her beautiful shoulders and the diamonds her mother had given her as a wedding present sparkled at her ears and at her neck.

Now that the champagne had chased away the butterflies that had been flitting about her stomach earlier in the evening,

Elizabeth was able to sit back and enjoy the urbane charm of Sir Edwin's conversation.

He talked to her about Vienna, about the woman's place in art, about the Liberal party and the Finance Bill, about 'The Wind in the Willows' and the new symphony by the new composer Elgar.

He probed and explored the inner recesses of Elizabeth's mind searching for the troubled places as a surgeon searches for a cancer in the body.

'You bear a great responsibility,' he told her. 'Like Dante's Beatrice or Shakespeare's Dark Lady.'

'They were not married,' Elizabeth replied. 'I fear the wife has to be content with the Second Best Bed.'

Sir Edwin was delighted.

'Witty, my dear! How could he fail to marry you when you pile wit and knowledge on top of beauty like Pelion upon Ossa?'

Elizabeth began to have the feeling that she had suddenly woken up to the enjoyment of civilisation after a long and horrible dream. No one had paid her that sort of a compliment for years. Sir Edwin mistook her look of surprise for one of censure at his flowery banter.

'It's a performance I've acquired to compensate for a hideous bashfulness,' he confessed. 'Beneath the peacock is a partridge and a very humble one. But if I let him out too often he'll be shot. Please be understanding and forgive me.'

'I think he's lovely,' Rose whispered to Thomas who was just returning from filling Sir Edwin's and Elizabeth's glasses.

'You take care, Rosie,' Thomas confided. 'He's an old fox. He'll have your chickens if you don't watch out!'

'You're a terror, Thomas Watkins,' said Rose.

'So is he, mark my words,' Thomas answered with a wink.

It was some time after one o'clock and most of the company had forgotten their high principles and were shouting out the chorus of 'Aunt Jemima', grouped round the upright piano in the drawing room when Elizabeth discovered that Sir Edwin was an expert on European porcelain. She told him that she had fallen in love with a piece of china on her honeymoon.

'The head of a child, in dreamy white porcelain,' she went on, her grammar becoming confused by the wine. 'And lovely Lawrence bought it for me.'

'Meissen we were told,' Lawrence explained.

'I must see it,' Sir Edwin demanded.

It was up in the bedroom but nothing would deter the connoisseur.

'Come, my children, lead me to it,' he demanded, putting an arm round each of them. 'I have not come all the way to Greenwich to be denied the sight of a fine piece of Meissen.'

It was not Meissen; it was not even porcelain; it was faience from Alcora in Spain.

'A rare and wonderful thing from the eighteenth century,' said Sir Edwin and as he went on to explain to Elizabeth the exact process by which the piece of faience had been made Lawrence withdrew below to entertain his guests, leaving his publisher to befriend his wife.

'You've gone very quiet all of a sudden,' said Rose to Thomas. It was nearly four o'clock in the morning and she was making herself a cup of cocoa before going to bed.

'There's been enough babble in this house tonight to last a week in Babylon,' Thomas answered her darkly.

'I don't know what you're going on about,' Rose answered, taking the saucepan of milk off the gas.

'Our respected employers,' Thomas explained, picking his teeth with a match. 'They're like two children playing with fire.'

'Just because they drunk a lot of bubbly and read out rhymes aloud,' said Rose.

'Oh you're too innocent, Rose.'

Thomas stood up and looked at the clock.

'I think I'll lie in tomorrow,' he said. 'Ask young Lawrence to lay out my dark clothes—I'm going to a funeral.'

'Your own most likely,' Rose retorted.

CHAPTER THREE

One hot, sticky, thundery August evening Colonel Winter of the Life Guards called on the Bellamys at 165 Eaton Place. Both Lady Marjorie and Richard knew the colonel slightly for he was their son James' commanding officer and although they guessed that it was on that account that he had come to see them, ensconced in the wing chair in the morning room, the colonel clearly found it difficult to come to the point. With some considerable pulling at his moustaches, he touched first on the weather, then on the state visit of the King and Queen of Spain later that month, a subject which led naturally on to the unfortunate outbreak of coughing that was affecting the horses of the Household Cavalry that summer.

In an attempt to ease the situation Richard suggested that the colonel might like to see him alone.

'No,' said Colonel Winter, taking a good pull at his whisky and clearing his throat. 'As you can probably guess, I've come to see you about your son and heir.'

Not knowing in the least what to expect Colonel Winter's next words came as an unpleasant shock.

'Well, not to mince matters,' the colonel continued speaking very much into his moustache, 'we're awfully worried about him.'

For a moment he seemed at a loss for words.

'As you know I think, we all think a lot of James. He's popular with the men and well liked in the mess.'

There was a difficult silence.

'We haven't seen very much of him since the regiment moved down to Windsor,' Richard explained.

'We were beginning to wonder how he was getting on,' Lady Marjorie added, more for something to say than anything else. Colonel Winter fidgeted and looked at his finger nails.

'I'm afraid I am getting awfully bad reports from the adjutant,' he said.

'What sort of reports?' Richard asked him.

'Well,' said the colonel, 'he's been reported twice for being in an unfit state when on duty as Squadron officer of the day; been returning to barracks at all times of the day and night, late for guard mounting—that sort of thing—and that's not all I'm afraid.'

Colonel Winter blew his nose and went on with the sad list: tradesmen coming down from London to serve writs; money owed to brother officers, even some trouble over a mess bill. It was only too clear that James was in serious trouble and that Colonel Winter was being as nice about it as he could.

'Sorry to bring you such rotten news,' he said. 'But we don't want a thing like this to get about, do we?'

The Bellamys emphatically did not want it to get about and they promised to take swift action to discipline their son and the colonel went off to join a party of friends to watch Mademoiselle Genée dance Coppelia at the Empire, much relieved that his ordeal was over.

Richard Bellamy was in a fury with his son for not coming

to see them and for generally behaving like a damn young idiot but Lady Marjorie was inclined to defend her ewe lamb and to search about for excuses. James hadn't wanted to worry them; he had fallen by bad luck into the wrong company or the clutches of some greedy unprincipled female who was taking him for every penny she could squeeze out of him.

If Lady Marjorie had but known it the clutches her son was in at that moment were those of one Sarah Moffat, a little chirpy music hall actress and once upon a time under house parlourmaid at 165 Eaton Place. They were together in a third class lodging house in Deptford which were Sarah's digs for the week and far from squeezing him for every penny she was offering him the last three sovereigns she had in the world until her salary was paid on Friday.

The truth was that James Bellamy had grown bored with the gay life and the endless parties and the glittering amusing women of his own age and had lost all interest in his regimental duties, seeing himself as nothing but a pawn in a costly and elaborate royal pageant. Not having the strength of character to throw it all up and start some other more interesting activity he had taken to gambling and to drinking and when these proved no solace had sought escape with Sarah.

James had been attracted to Sarah ever since he had first seen her cleaning the stairs at his parents' home five years before. When she had left he had kept in touch with her, but it was not till he had met her again at Elizabeth's wedding and in a fit of euphoria brought on by the champagne promised to take her to Paris, that the relationship could have been said to have become serious.

The Paris trip had been a wonderful success. Sarah had given herself completely to James and had fallen in love with him. It had also been extremely expensive and James found himself getting deeper and deeper into debt and gambling for higher and higher stakes. Only in Sarah's company did he find he could still relax and forget his troubles.

'Thank God for you, Sarah,' he said.

'Please don't mention it, I'm sure,' Sarah replied, using her Special Posh voice which she knew always amused him.

'Sorry it can't be Romano's tonight,' James said apologetically.

'Here, you remember that place with all the mirrors,' said Sarah. 'Chez Maxim's; well we're dining "Chez Moi" tonight. I got a couple of kippers in the larder and a pint of wallop in the jug.'

Seeing he still looked rather despondent Sarah made a face.

'Cheer up, Captain, there's a good boy. You're not dead till you're buried.' She particularly wanted him to be on good form that evening; but it was gong to be hard work she could see that.

'Just let me get my hat off,' she went on, pulling out the long hat pin and taking off her big flowered hat, 'and then . . . and then' she hissed, 'who knows what devilish goings-on may take place at number fifteen Dock Street, Deptford? Where Lord James Bellamy is keeping a secret rendezvous with the woman of his dreams; her as lies curled up on the tiger skin, panting, voluptuous, dangerous.'

She poured out a glass of the beer and offered it to James.

'The better to enflame the young nobleman's passions,' she purred. James smiled and Sarah was happy.

After their humble supper James went round to the off licence and bought a bottle of gin and after a bit they started to rag about and sing and as usual the woman above started banging on the ceiling.

'Shut up you noisy old bag,' Sarah shouted and James shook his fists in the air. When he turned round there was no sign of Sarah.

She had fallen behind the table in a dead faint.

He carried her to the bed and bathed her forehead and in a few moments Sarah came round.

'It all went dizzy and black,' she said weakly.

It would have been easy to have blamed the hot night and the gin for her collapse but he had to be told sometime.

'We're in the soup proper, Jimmy,' she admitted. 'Cos . . . well, there's a little captain on the way.'

James just stared at her. He wasn't expecting anything like this.

'A little James Bellamy inside me,' Sarah went on, still trying to put it as lightly as she could. 'It means I shan't be able to work much longer.'

James didn't say a word, but he looked completely shattered. It was hard to take such a new knock at a time like this and it was no comfort that it was all his fault.

'You mustn't be angry,' Sarah pleaded, 'because it's your little one that's coming, yours and mine, Jimmy, there's been no one else, on my word of honour. So don't be angry. I couldn't bear it if you was angry.'

James wasn't angry, he was desperate.

Sarah wasn't going to give up.

'Here give us the bottle,' she said. James handed her the gin.

'Mother's ruin,' she began, and put her hand to her mouth in horror at what she had said.

The next morning Sarah felt horribly ill and very miserable and very lonely. It wasn't that James had been unkind to her, it wasn't that she had expected him to rush into marrying her, but she hadn't expected him to be quite so . . . non-committal. It had been a silly time to tell him, she saw that now, both of them half sodden with gin. She wondered what she should do. Unlike James Bellamy who had a mother and father and a family, Sarah had no real friends in the world, no family, no real friends anywhere except Rose. Rose hadn't always approved of Sarah, quite often she had not approved of Sarah at all, but Rose was the sort you could talk to.

Sarah knew that Rose went up to Eaton Place from Greenwich every week regularly and Deptford was almost on her way. Rose answered her call the very next week.

'I'm in such trouble, Rose,' Sarah confessed to her friend. 'Help me. What am I to do?'

'What to do?' Rose answered sharply. 'It's what he's got to do, more like. Marry you of course, and keep you.'

It was crystal clear to Rose that James Bellamy, as an officer and a gentleman, was honour bound to support Sarah.

'He's got to see you through all right and if he hasn't got any money he'll just have to get some from the Master and Lady Marjorie. They'll have to—well do something about it; after all he's their son, and you was their servant—once. They'll have to know, Sarah, whatever happens.'

Sarah made a face.

'And if he won't tell them then you'll have to.'

'Oh no,' said Sarah, most unwilling to agree to anything that would hurt her lover.

'If he tells them he'll get into awful trouble,' she explained, 'and he's been very good to me, Rosie.'

'Good to you, has he,' Rose replied bitterly. 'Landing you in this muck.'

'I'm fond of him, Rose, for all his faults,' Sarah continued. 'He's nice, Jimmy is. He's . . . nice.'

Rose shook her head. 'You're a hopeless case, Sarah,' she said. 'That's what you are. Hopeless.'

She stroked Sarah's hair just as she used to do in their little attic bedroom at 165 Eaton Place whenever Sarah had been unhappy and upset.

'Thank you for coming, Rosie,' said Sarah. 'I feel no end bucked up.'

As it happened the rapid march of events spared Sarah the necessity of carrying out Rose's advice to the letter. Even as Rose was climbing onto the tram that for the price of three farthings would clank and bang its way over Deptford Bridge and along the High Street to Greenwich and deposit her at the bottom of the hill, James Bellamy was entering his parents' house for the most important meeting of his life.

Seated in the morning room he catalogued his debts for the benefit of his parents. They were not as large or as disastrous as either of the Bellamys had suspected.

'I'm sorry. I'm in a dreadful mess,' James admitted, and Lady Marjorie looked almost relieved.

'Yes, you are,' said Richard, flatly determined not to be soft with his son.

'Why didn't you come and tell us?' Lady Marjorie pleaded. 'We could have helped.'

James nodded. 'I'm supposed to be independent, you know. I've got an allowance from you—and my pay.'

'Evidently not enough for the kind of life you are leading,' Richard commented sourly.

Now that the issue was fairly joined it seemed to James that the moment had come to take the plunge.

'That's really what I wanted to speak to you about,' he said. 'You see it's all connected with something else. A rather delicate personal matter.'

'A woman I suppose?' said Lady Marjorie.

James nodded. Lady Marjorie had guessed all the time that there was a woman involved but when she and her husband heard the woman's name and the true nature of the trouble they were completely dumbfounded.

'Sarah's on the stage,' James told them. 'Or was. Of course she can't go on with it now because . . . well, because of this baby, of which I am the father.' He made a helpless gesture with his hands. 'Now you know everything.'

In the silence that followed the clock on the mantelshelf striking the hour seemed almost deafening.

'There's trouble, Mrs Bridges,' Mr Hudson confided to the cook. 'Over money again if you ask me. That young shaver's got himself into debt again.'

Mrs Bridges nodded. It was perfectly normal in her experience for young gentlemen to get into debt through women and gambling and as far as she was concerned reflected no discredit on the son of the house—rather the reverse.

'Saucy monkey,' she said. 'Is that what the trouble is about? Well, it's in the blood. There was his great uncle Bertie, you remember, old Lady Southwold's youngest brother; him as lost all his money at Monte Carlo and died of the shingles in Bordigheria.'

Her memory of the minutiae of the scandals of the past was always very impressive if not strictly accurate in detail.

'He'll talk himself out of it, that young man,' she added. ''Specially where her ladyship's concerned. She thinks the sun shines out of his eyes. He can't do no wrong can't Captain James . . . not so far as her ladyship's concerned . . .'

This time the crime was too great for even Lady Marjorie to condone. There was the danger of a major family scandal and that was something that could neither be glossed over or hidden away. Action would have to be taken.

Over the coffee James was sworn to a complete silence and sent back to Windsor to await events.

'I don't know what to say, Mother,' he said to Lady Marjorie as he left. 'Except that I am very sorry to disgrace you like this. Very sorry.'

Lady Marjorie was clearly distressed but like a true patrician she showed no sign of it.

'I'm glad you had the courage to tell us the truth, my darling,' she said quietly. 'That's the important thing.'

In the cab and later in the train from Paddington down to Windsor James turned over the facts of the day in his mind. He felt an enormous sense of relief and of emptiness. He knew that whatever happened next would be decided for him by the forces of law and order within the Southwold family. There would be a meeting, probably that evening and most certainly in a London club or at the House of

Lords, a meeting that would be presided over by his grand-father, the old Earl of Southwold with his father and Sir Geoffrey Dillon, the family solicitor, also present. Sir Geoffrey would know what to do, he always did, and cases such as this one were by no means uncommon in Edwardian London. In any case the responsibility no longer rested with Captain James Bellamy.

In forty-eight hours all the arrangements had been made to cope with the situation. It only remained for the principal actors in the drama to be instructed in the parts they were to play.

Mr Hudson's evasive and uncertain manner during serv-ants' hall dinner and then the arrival in quick succession at the front door of Sir Geoffrey Dillon followed by Captain James confirmed Mrs Bridges in her suspicion that some-thing fishy was going on, but she was not prepared for what was to follow.

Rose appeared on the area steps followed by Sarah carry-ing a large suitcase.

'Back door, Ruby, if you please,' said Mr Hudson, look-ing at his watch and turning to the others. 'I would appreciate it if you would refrain from asking too many questions, for the time being,' he said.

Rose came into the servants' hall followed by Sarah. All eyes were upon her as Mr Hudson sat her down at the long table.

'Wotcher, Sarah,' said Edward. 'Everything all right?'

Mr Hudson decided to drop another fillip of information.

'Her Ladyship and Sir Geoffrey wish to interview Sarah upstairs,' he told them.

If anything this remark served to increase the curiosity of the other servants. When Mr Hudson went to his pantry to get his tail coat, Mrs Bridges turned to Rose.

'Where do you come in, Rose?' she asked.

Rose looked uneasy.

'Well her ladyship asked Miss Lizzie if she could spare me for the day to fetch Sarah from her lodgings and bring her here,' she explained. 'Isn't that right, Sarah?'

'That's right,' said Sarah.

'Seeing as we're old friends and I knew where she was living,' Rose went on. 'Isn't that right, Sarah?'

'That's right,' said Sarah.

Mrs Bridges sniffed. She didn't like being played with. If there was one thing that annoyed Mrs Bridges it was people having secrets behind her back.

'Not exactly full of chat like you used to be when you was in service,' she said to Sarah.

'I'm not very well,' Sarah explained, very weak and pathetic.

Mrs Bridges was puzzled. She remembered Sarah and her lies.

'Well, I'm sorry to hear that,' she replied in her most non-committal voice. 'Captain James is up in the morning room,' she added, pointedly fishing, but Sarah didn't seem to hear her, she was gazing intently round the servants' hall.

'Not changed much has it, this room?' she remarked to the company in general.

'Nothing changes at 165,' Mr Hudson answered as he came back into the room and looked at Sarah over his glasses. 'Except the staff.'

The morning room bell rang and made Sarah jump. It was the summons. As she followed the butler up the stone backstairs that she had once known so well she wished she was still the under house parlourmaid just going up to turn down the beds.

In the servants' hall Mrs Bridges determined to stand no more nonsense from Rose. She dismissed the younger servants and turned to her.

'Now Rose, what's it all about, eh?'

Rose shrugged and twisted her fingers together.

'I don't know as I ought to say, Mrs Bridges,' she explained. 'I mean if it got round other servants' halls . . .'

Mrs Bridges tucked in her chin crossly. 'If it concerns the family,' she said firmly, 'it concerns me, Rose.'

'Yes Mrs Bridges,' Rose replied weakly.

In the front hall Sarah stopped and looked round. 'Here,' she said to Mr Hudson, 'do you remember the first time I ever came in here?'

The butler remembered the occasion only too clearly. 'Your face when I tried to come in through the front door,' said Sarah laughing. 'And then you said I wasn't to question my betters and you was my better because you was older and wiser—and I was to learn humility. Remember?'

'It's a pity you didn't learn it,' said Mr Hudson gravely as he led the way across to the morning room door.

Sarah followed, thinking that she had never seen Mr Hudson laugh. Not so much as once.

'Put your hat straight,' he ordered when they were outside the door.

Sarah straightened the extraordinary confection of straw and feathers that served as her hat.

'Lead me to the slaughter,' she said as gaily as she could manage.

Mr Hudson opened the door. 'Sarah, m'lady,' he announced.

Lady Marjorie was sitting on the sofa and James beyond by his mother's desk. Richard Bellamy and a formidable man in black who Sarah presumed to be Sir Geoffrey Dillon were standing in front of the fire. Sarah advanced holding up her chin under her ridiculous hat.

Richard Bellamy opened the batting. 'Sit down, Sarah,' he said in a friendly, easy sort of way and Sarah sat down cautiously and with enormous dignity.

'I'll be brief,' Richard went on, pursing his lips. 'My son has . . . er told us of your . . . your friendship with him, since you left our employ and . . . and of your present condition resulting from that relationship.'

He thought he had put it rather neatly.

'Yes, sir,' Sarah assented.

'It goes without saying that we, as a family, accept absolutely our responsibility for your future.'

Sarah nodded; it was certainly better than anything she had expected.

'I don't want to make any trouble for anyone, honest,' she explained with a touch of magnanimity brought on by a feeling of relief. 'It was my fault as much as Captain James'. It's just that with the baby coming and everything, I can't work you see no more and I haven't got any money . . . not to bring up the baby like it should be brought up, seeing it's your grandchild, m'lady.'

She put her hand to her mouth as soon as the words were out wishing she hadn't spoken.

43

'Keep your big mouth shut,' had been Rose's advice and Rose was right.

'Quite,' said Richard Bellamy, breaking the awkward silence. It might have been the signal for Sir Geoffrey Dillon, who stood up and took over the situation with a calm precision born of many years of experience of such difficult domestic situations.

Quietly he explained the details of registering a child born out of wedlock; he made it sound like buying a postal order. Sarah listened carefully and with interest. Dillon noted that she seemed relaxed.

'Now, Sarah,' he continued in a friendly almost paternal manner, 'arrangements have been made for you to travel at once to Southwold, Lady Marjorie's family estate where you will be lodged with a Mr and Mrs Clay at their cottage. You will find them an agreeable and homely couple, Mr Clay being head gamekeeper to Lord Southwold and Mrs Clay, by good fortune, a qualified midwife.'

'Here, just a minute,' said Sarah. Her head was in a whirl.

'Let Sir Geoffrey continue, Sarah,' said Richard Bellamy. 'It's for your own good.' And Sir Geoffrey did continue pouring out a string of factual suggestions which covered the birth of the baby, its upbringing, schooling and possible career as well as her own future position in the laundry at Southwold.

Sarah felt her whole world slipping away.

'Look Mister,' she said. 'I'm not going to be stuck away in some rotten cottage in the middle of nowhere with people I've never even seen before just because . . .'

'Sarah,' Lady Marjorie interrupted sharply. 'Everything possible is being done to ensure your comfort and welfare.'

'I think you should realise,' Sir Geoffrey continued, 'that marriage to the father of the child would be quite out of the question.'

She hadn't accepted that fact at all, in fact she had been banking on it, and now she looked across at James Bellamy. He gave her no comfort.

'I think you have been in domestic service long enough to know that,' Sir Geoffrey added.

'I'm not a housemaid now,' Sarah reminded him sharply. 'I'm an actress. On the stage. I'm respectable.'

'I'm sorry to disillusion you,' Sir Geoffrey answered patiently, 'but the acting profession is not generally considered respectable.'

'Oh isn't it,' Sarah was really angry now. 'Well perhaps you don't know it but there's plenty of actresses what has married famous men—peers of the realm and all. There's Rosie Boot, and Denise Orme and some wot's only in the chorus.'

As often when her passions were aroused Sarah's grammar suffered accordingly.

It was a brave performance and James bowed his head in misery at Sir Geoffrey's inevitable reply.

'Nevertheless, officers in the Household Brigade are not permitted to marry actresses.'

Sarah frowned; it sounded far fetched and James had never spoken to her about it.

She looked over at him. 'Is that true?' she asked. James confirmed it with a sad nod of his head.

'If Captain Bellamy was to offer you his hand in marriage,' Sir Geoffrey continued with inexorable logic, 'he would be obliged to resign his commission in the Life Guards.'

He made it sound a fate akin to public hanging.

'I didn't know that,' Sarah replied on the retreat.

'I'm sure you wouldn't want to destroy his career, would you, Sarah?' Sir Geoffrey asked almost gently.

'I don't know,' said Sarah near to tears. She was beaten; there were too many big guns against her.

'Why don't you say something, Jimmy?' Sarah appealed in desperation. 'I don't expect you to marry me. But you might say something.'

But James had been sworn to silence. Sir Geoffrey delivered the coup de grace in the same level voice devoid of any emotion.

'Captain Bellamy has given his parents an undertaking neither to see you or to attempt to communicate with you ever again. I must ask for a similar undertaking from you.'

Sarah stood up to her full height of five foot four. She was determined not to show them how she felt inside. Her instinct was to tell them just what she thought of them but she had learnt that this would do no good to anyone least of all herself.

'If there's nothing else, m'lady,' Sarah said to Lady Marjorie with enormous dignity, 'I'll go downstairs, and sit with my friends, until it's time to go.'

She gave one last look across at James Bellamy and then turned and went through the door and shut it behind her.

In spite of his father's efforts to restrain him, James followed her.

'Sarah, wait!' he called to her across the hall. 'I'll . . . I'll write to you,' he added lamely. Sarah went through the green baize door without a word. James shrugged to himself. What could he do or what could he say? They were both puppets in a play over which neither of them had any control.

He turned back slowly towards the morning room. As he opened the door he felt a strong desire to run away.

'Well that all seemed perfectly satisfactory,' said Sir Geoffrey. 'Now James, we can discuss your future.' He looked at James over his glasses.

'What is there to discuss?' Lady Marjorie asked suspiciously.

Sir Geoffrey explained that arrangements had been made for James to be seconded to an Indian cavalry regiment called the Scinde Horse which was then stationed in Peshawar. The P & O boat that would be taking him to the east would be leaving England on the sixteenth of the month.

'Have you gone out of your mind, Sir Geoffrey?' Lady Marjorie demanded. 'This is quite unthinkable.'

Lady Marjorie wanted to know who had first suggested the extraordinary idea that her son should be banished in the first place. She was absolutely furious that any arrangements had been made behind her back. It was disloyal of her husband and impudent of a man who after all was nothing but the family solicitor.

In the middle of this battle over his person, James slipped out to begin his packing.

'I am the family lawyer and I must advise well,' Sir Geoffrey explained to Lady Marjorie. 'After all the family name must be protected at all times from scandal. I think James himself recognises that.'

'James may recognise that but I do not,' Lady Marjorie spat back at him. 'I want it clearly understood Sir Geoffrey that I absolutely forbid you to proceed with these arrangements until I have talked to my father.'

'Perhaps I ought to point out, Lady Marjorie,' Sir Geoffrey replied, 'that it was your father who consulted the Viceroy concerning the choice of regiment for your son.'

The solicitor allowed no hint of triumph to creep into his voice.

'It was a happy chance,' he went on, 'that Lord Southwold and Lord Minto were such old friends.'

Lady Marjorie was silent. Hardly ever in her life had she been so put down before.

Richard apologised for his wife's discourtesy as Edward helped Sir Geoffrey with his coat and hat and stick.

'A lioness protecting her young is entitled to show her claws. I respect that,' said Sir Geoffrey. He admired Lady Marjorie enormously; there were not so many real ladies left. 'India may well be the making of your son,' he added. Edward, at the door, pricked his ears.

'Thank you for all you have done,' Richard said. 'It can't have been easy.'

Sir Geoffrey Dillon allowed himself a fleeting smile.

'My dear Richard,' he said, 'that is precisely why we solicitors charge such exorbitant fees.'

He went down the steps where his carriage was waiting. Sir Geoffrey was old fashioned about his means of transportation.

The news that Captain James was going to India, brought downstairs by Edward, caused a sensation in the servants' hall and removed Sarah's last seed of hope. When the cab arrived she followed Rose silently up the area steps to the street.

'I don't know what will become of that poor child, really I don't,' said Mrs Bridges who had a kind and forgiving heart. Mr Hudson sniffed. 'Good riddance, if you ask me,' he said.

On the way across the Park to Paddington Station, Sarah held Rose's hand tight.

'Rose, I'm frightened,' she admitted.

CHAPTER FOUR

Elizabeth went with her parents to Tilbury to see her brother off to India. Everyone was very jolly and gay and as they walked round admiring the great liner with its wooden shutters and fans and dark-skinned crew which already gave a flavour of the East to that rainy English day, Elizabeth felt a strong desire to hide herself away somewhere, to escape from the suburban house that she was already beginning to think of as a prison.

Her brief experience in the arms of the publisher on the night of the soirée had been no cure for the illness that beset her marriage. For a few hours it had abated the fever but it had left Elizabeth with a deep sense of guilt, of having connived with Lawrence at an act of degradation, but above all, it had removed her innocence. Elizabeth had eaten of the apple and she now knew what Lawrence was unwilling or unable to give her.

Rose and Thomas watched sadly as their master and mistress drew further apart. The least trivial incident, the cooking of an egg, the colour of a piece of wool, the state of the weather could cause an instant flare up, but these were mere skirmishes, there were no more battles. The battle was already lost and as the leaves in Greenwich Park turned from green to gold and fell in great swirling sprays before the western winds of November, Lawrence and Elizabeth's marriage was dying with them.

Thomas did his best to divert them and alleviate their suffering. He was always cheery and pleasant to Lawrence who became very fond of his valet and came to look on him as a friend. Thomas suggested to Elizabeth that she should buy a small motor car to allow herself more freedom to get out into the world. The suggestion was not entirely altruistic for Thomas was passionately devoted to the internal combustion engine. Ever since his younger days in his father's bicycle shop in South Wales he had been a good mechanic and by dint of hard application had turned himself into a good driver with a sound knowledge of the most intricate details of the modern automobile.

Elizabeth was delighted with the motor of Thomas' choice, a Dennis tourer, second hand, for only two hundred pounds. She insisted on learning to drive it herself and became quite a terror to the pedestrians of Blackheath, ending up one afternoon with a hectic swerve off the road over the grass with the two front wheels in a pond.

'Stunning!' Elizabeth observed very flushed and excited. 'I just need to master the steering. Funny such a little movement makes it go such a long way.'

'Yes, madam,' Thomas agreed succinctly, very glad to be still in one piece.

'You were nervous, Thomas, weren't you?' his mistress sounded amused. 'I found it exhilarating.'

'Exhilarating!' Thomas repeated with feeling. 'The very word for it. It'll be a flying machine next.'

It was true. Elizabeth would very much have liked to have driven an aeroplane and hadn't Mr Wright been off the ground for four minutes and fifteen seconds at a height of ten feet that very September?

Whenever Lady Marjorie came out to visit her daughter in Greenwich she found what was apparently a contented, happy household. Elizabeth was the perfect hostess and both Rose and Thomas were attentive to the important visitor on these occasions. Thomas especially took every opportunity to make the best of himself. As usual he had a very good reason. It was the big blue Renault car that had brought Lady Marjorie and was standing outside the house. Thomas despised old Mr Pearce, the Bellamy's coachman now turned chauffeur for neither knowing or caring what went on beneath the brass bonnet of the car and he envied him his smart uniform with the shiny black leggings and the cockade in his cap. Thomas had set his mind on taking Mr Pearce's place and he bided his time knowing that a break up must come to the Kirbridge household sooner or later.

He hadn't long to wait. Lawrence had moved into his dressing room and a system of remote communication had been evolved whereby Lawrence would give Thomas a message who would transfer it to Rose who would then pass it on to Elizabeth.

It was by this means that Elizabeth discovered in mid-December that Lawrence was about to depart to stay with an aunt and would probably prolong his visit over Christmas. The thought of Christmas alone at Greenwich appalled her and drove her to make the decision so long put off.

It was Elizabeth's day to have tea at Eaton Place with her parents but the eagle eye of Mr Hudson immediately detected something odd about the amount of luggage the footman and Thomas were bringing into the house from the car.

'There's been a change of plan,' Rose explained obliquely.

Lady Marjorie was delighted to have her daughter to stay for Christmas, or as long as she liked, but she, like Mr Hudson, found it strange that the newly married couple should be spending the feast apart.

Wisely she waited for Elizabeth to explain the situation in her own good time.

Over dinner Richard told his daughter that there had been good news from India. James was proving a success in the Scinde Horse and had already made his name in the regimental polo team. Lady Marjorie expressed the hope that James might pick on any of the eligible young ladies who yearly went East in search of a change and a husband, 'the fishing fleet' as they were called by the irreverent males.

'It's a marvellous chance for them,' said Lady Marjorie. 'Felicity Davenport landed a major.'

'Good for Felicity,' said Elizabeth brightly. 'What did he weigh?' They were eating fish.

'Darling,' Lady Marjorie replied, hoping Elizabeth wasn't in one of her silly moods.

'Well,' Elizabeth went on, 'you make him sound like a prize trout. What would James be, a sort of eel?'

'And Lawrence,' said Richard joining in the game, 'what would he be?'

Lady Marjorie tried to flash her husband a look of warning but he wasn't looking.

He had come back late after a long session at the House and she hadn't been able to tell him of her suspicions.

'Lawrence,' said Elizabeth thoughtfully, 'I think I see Lawrence as a plaice.'

Mr Hudson looked quickly across at Edward, who was serving the hock. Edward's lower lip quivered but no more.

'A plaice,' said Richard, 'why a plaice?'

'I don't know why. I just see him as one.'

'Well I don't think it's very illuminating,' said Lady Marjorie. 'I think it's a silly game.' She tried to steer the conversation into safer channels, but in no time her husband was asking Elizabeth about Lawrence's poetry and how he liked living in Greenwich.

'He isn't writing poetry any more,' Elizabeth replied, dangerously calm, 'and apparently Greenwich stifles him.'

'Stifles him?' Richard asked in genuine surprise. 'Why?'

'Well it probably wouldn't stifle you, papa . . . but I don't know why, it does Lawrence.'

'I thought I'd do some Christmas shopping tomorrow, darling,' Lady Marjorie said to Elizabeth, wishing she was near enough to kick her husband under the table. 'Will you come with me? We can give each other ideas, like we used to. Do you remember making those lists for everyone?'

'I don't want to be little again, mother,' Elizabeth replied ungraciously. There was a moment of awkward silence.

'I don't think your mother meant . . .' Richard began.

'Oh yes, she did,' Elizabeth interrupted. 'She sees my marriage in ruins and she wants to protect me by making me little again.'

Richard looked up at his wife in shocked surprise.

'What on earth?' he said weakly.

'It's plain enough. Haven't you guessed? I've given you all enough hints.' Elizabeth went on, only just in control. 'What do you think I'm doing here?' she demanded, her voice rising.

'Darling, please,' Lady Marjorie begged, looking quickly round. 'Pas devant les domestiques.'

54

Elizabeth shrugged and looked at Rose.

'Rose sait bien la situation,' she replied. 'And so do the others now.'

Afterwards Hudson was proud that neither Edward nor Rose had shown the least indication that they were listening.

'I can't believe it,' said Lady Marjorie in a voice of pain. 'After only six months, I mean . . .'

'Well of course you can't believe it, mother,' Elizabeth replied angrily. 'You don't want to believe it. You'll have to face the gossip and sniggering of your friends. But can't you think beyond that?' She stood up and threw down her napkin. 'Can't you think of me for once?' she shouted and ran out of the room slamming the door. In the silence that followed, Mr Hudson made a motion with his head releasing Rose to go upstairs while he and Edward went round collecting the dirty plates.

Rose found her young mistress lying on her bed. The fact that Elizabeth wasn't crying should have warned her that it would be better to leave her alone.

'Don't be upset, Miss Lizzie,' said Rose. 'I'm sure it's not as bad as you think. You've got it out of proportion.'

Rose's comforting voice served only to infuriate Elizabeth. The pent-up emotions of months came pouring out. She had held herself in for so long that it was a relief to be able to shout at someone.

'Don't tell me Rose!'

Rose persisted. 'Miss Lizzie . . .' she said.

'And don't call me Miss Lizzie. I'm a married woman. Married. Which is more than you'll ever be.'

Rose recoiled at the fierce cruelty of the attack.

'At least I've tried,' Elizabeth went on. 'I've offered myself. But you . . . you've never offered yourself to anyone. Oh I've heard you with Thomas . . . teasing and then stopping.'

She jumped up and faced Rose.

'Let me tell you, Rose, unless you're prepared to give yourself utterly and risk making a fool of yourself, you'll never get anything in life. You'll end up withered here inside.' She made a gesture that made Rose turn away.

'Look at you already,' Elizabeth added pointing at the maid, 'at least I'll never end up like you!'

Thomas was ready to take the car back to Greenwich. He looked in at the servants' hall and saw Rose sitting alone looking at the fire.

'Good night, Rosie,' he called.

Rose did not turn and he went over to her sensing something was wrong.

'What's the matter? What is it love?' he asked very tender and concerned as she turned her head from him.

'It's not what happened at dinner, is it?' he asked. 'We knew that was finished. We've got other fish to fry.'

'It isn't that . . .' Rose managed to mutter.

'Well what then?' Thomas took her hand.

'All our years together,' Rose sobbed. 'All the things we've shared, and then to say such hurtful things . . .'

'What things?'

He tried to take her other hand but she broke away and went quickly out of the room past Mr Hudson who was standing in the door watching them.

Thomas got up and went to Mr Hudson, who eyed him suspiciously.

'Rose. She seems a bit upset . . .' he explained, suddenly realising the butler was thinking the worst.

'It wasn't me, Mr Hudson . . .'

'Good-night.' Mr Hudson's voice was icy.

Richard Bellamy poured himself a whisky and soda and lit the second cigar of the evening. His doctor wouldn't have approved of it but he had had a long and difficult day and nothing, not even the most hard fought and bitter debate, exhausted and upset him so much as a family row, and just lately he seemed to have been exposed to more than his full share.

After dinner he had had a long and difficult discussion with his wife. Lady Marjorie, not without reason, had argued that Elizabeth should be sent packing back to Greenwich and told not to be so silly.

'All she needs is a good spanking,' Lady Marjorie had said. 'All her life she's been spoilt.' And here she had looked accusingly at her husband. 'All she has to do is throw a tantrum and immediately everyone gives in to her. I mean they were only married in June. I've never heard such a thing.'

But Richard hadn't been so sure. It had been Lady Marjorie who had taken her son's side when there was trouble and now, as always, Richard was prepared to stand by his daughter or at least find out more facts before coming to a decision.

He well knew that it was the aristocratic and conservative tradition so well embodied by his wife's family to endure endless years of unhappiness rather than allow the break-

57

down of a marriage. Richard himself was of a more liberal persuasion. He had seen families where husband and wife had not so much as spoken for years, but who had stayed together, 'for the children's sake', it was said. He had not seen any happiness resulting from it and anyway in this case there were no children. He had gone up to his daughter's room to talk to her and had gently probed her wounded soul. Elizabeth had not been exactly specific and Richard had not pressed her, but he had come away convinced that at least in Elizabeth's mind the marriage was in ruins and could never be built up again. He felt it was reasonable grounds to call in Sir Geoffrey Dillon once again as family counsellor and advisor. He would more easily find out the facts and tell them if there was indeed a possible legal solution to the problem.

Elizabeth had always lived in awe of Sir Geoffrey, in fact it had always been a secret joke between James and herself that his real source of revenue was a factory which turned babies into candles by a boiling and refining process known only to himself.

As she sat facing him in the morning room the thin lips and the cold piercing eyes through the gold-rimmed spectacles put her in mind of her childhood fantasies. Strangely enough, if she had only known it, Sir Geoffrey was himself unusually ill at ease. He was a dedicated bachelor and extremely fastidious in his habits and in spite of long practice always found the intimate details of his clients' private lives difficult to discuss.

'Well,' he began, 'er . . . Mrs Kirbridge . . .'

'Elizabeth,' said Elizabeth. 'Please. Since you've known me since the day I was born.'

'Elizabeth,' said Sir Geoffrey. 'Though I regret my knowledge of you is confined to a handful of dry facts . . . date of birth, that sort of thing.'

'Well,' she replied, 'doubtless you mean to change all that.' Sir Geoffrey looked puzzled.

'Aren't I supposed to use you as a sort of father confessor . . . tell you the intimate details I wouldn't even tell my parents?'

'Well,' said Sir Geoffrey.

'If the law requires, then let's get it over.'

Sir Geoffrey opened his despatch case and took out a notebook. At least the girl sounded practical. After some preliminary skirmishing he came to the point.

'A woman can divorce her husband on grounds of adultery coupled with desertion or adultery coupled with cruelty,' he explained carefully.

'You mean we choose one of those?' Elizabeth asked.

Sir Geoffrey wouldn't have put it that way.

'In effect,' he said, 'we decide on relevant grounds.'

'Well, neither of those is relevant.'

'There is of course the possibility of an annulment,' said Sir Geoffrey. 'Grounds for which can be to take an example: impotence of the husband . . .'

He was about to continue when a slight gesture and a look of doubt on Elizabeth's face told him that he was on the right line, however faint the scent.

'Think carefully,' he said quietly, 'might that be relevant?'

Elizabeth thought that it might. The trouble was she wasn't sure exactly what it meant.

Sir Geoffrey explained to her in as clinical and technical

terms as was possible, exactly the legal definition of male impotence. After that she was silent.

'Do you understand?' he asked her.

'Yes. Yes. I understand,' Elizabeth replied. Please let me sink through the floor, she thought, must I tell this old ogre everything?

'Nothing ever happened,' she blurted out suddenly.

Sir Geoffrey coughed.

'Well if your husband was impotent it wouldn't.'

'No, I don't mean that,' Elizabeth went on desperately.

'You're saying, Elizabeth,' Sir Geoffrey said crisply, 'that sexual intercourse has never taken place between you and your husband.'

Elizabeth nodded.

Sir Geoffrey looked across at Elizabeth. He was no great expert in these matters but his eyes told him that he was looking at an extremely attractive young woman.

'You've . . . er . . . you've shown yourself willing,' he asked with an embarrassed cough. 'You've encouraged him . . . but . . . er . . .'

'Yes, yes,' Elizabeth blurted out, looking down at her hands. 'He seems to find the act repugnant, that's what he says.'

Sir Geoffrey hoped she wouldn't start to weep; it tended to blur the true facts.

'But how can he?' Elizabeth pleaded. 'I am not repugnant to him, not in our normal life. But when I lie beside him in bed and reach out for him, he doesn't . . .' she shook her head sadly. 'He doesn't seem . . .'

Sir Geoffrey coughed again, he was not by his nature a father confessor.

'I see . . .' he said quickly. 'Thank you,' and then shut his notebook with a snap. 'Well I think we have the grounds.'

Elizabeth was surprised; it had all seemed easier than she had expected.

'Of course there will have to be a simple medical inspection.'

'Medical inspection!' Elizabeth asked with a note of panic in her voice. 'Of whom?'

'Of both of you,' Sir Geoffrey explained. 'I'll speak to your mother. It needn't concern you.'

'But it does concern me,' Elizabeth maintained. 'I'm the one that is being examined.'

Sir Geoffrey Dillon smiled as kindly as he could.

'Don't be alarmed, my dear,' he said. 'It's a formality. Now shall we call your mother?'

'What are young fellows coming to these days!' Richard Bellamy exclaimed, at his most parliamentary pompous when he heard the news.

'Wretched boy!' said Lady Marjorie. 'He must have known he couldn't come up to scratch. He should never have married her. Poor darling girl.'

There was some comfort in being righteously indignant with hindsight and some relief that it was not their daughter's fault.

Thomas had been to 165 Eaton Place with a further consignment of luggage and as he had done full justice to Mrs Bridges' high tea it was dark by the time he got back to the house at Greenwich. He was surprised and somewhat alarmed to see lights on in the hall and the bedroom. Inside he found his master sitting on the bed drinking champagne.

'All gone, eh Thomas?' said Lawrence. 'All my pretty chickens at one fell swoop . . .'

'Yes sir,' Thomas replied, non-committal, wondering how best to act in the circumstances. 'Will you be staying, sir?' he asked.

'Yes, of course I'll be staying. I live here, Thomas.' He stared moodily at the bed. 'Do you want some champagne?'

'No thank you, sir.'

'Why not?' Lawrence was belligerent at once.

'Well, sir, if you insist,' Thomas agreed, prepared to sail with the prevailing wind.

'I don't insist,' Lawrence sounded infinitely tired and weary. 'Have some if you want some. Don't if you don't.'

Thomas went to the bathroom and fetched a glass and drank some champagne.

'It's not unpleasant, sir,' said Thomas politely.

'It damn well shouldn't be,' Lawrence replied. 'My aunt knows about these things.'

'I trust,' Thomas ventured, 'I trust your aunt has not been taken sick?'

'Why should she . . . ?' Lawrence looked up blankly.

'. . . necessitating your unexpected return,' Thomas explained.

'Necessitating my unexpected,' Lawrence mimicked. 'You're getting pedantic, Thomas. Who taught you to speak like that? Hudson, the Scotsman? Only servile servants speak like that, and you're not one of them.'

'Am I not, sir?' Thomas answered, rather pleased.

'You know you're not,' said Lawrence looking more cheerful. 'I came back, because I was feeling wretched. I missed my wife's company. Do you believe that?'

'Yes, sir.'

'Then you're a fool. A fool, Thomas.'

Lawrence refilled the tooth glass. 'I returned for an assignation with another lady which requires your utmost discretion. Do you believe that?'

'No, sir,' said Thomas humouring.

'No, sir? Why not, sir?' demanded Lawrence.

'Well . . .' said Thomas. 'Because . . .'

'Because you think I'm a homosexual?'

It was a word that had come into common if not into polite use with the trial of Oscar Wilde.

'No, sir,' Thomas was indignant.

'What? What do you think, man? For God's sake say what you think.' Lawrence, excited by the wine, began to pace about the room. Thomas remained remarkably cool.

'I think,' he said slowly, 'I think you're a romantic.'

'Romantic?' Lawrence was rather tickled. 'What do you know about romantics?'

'I read books,' Thomas explained.

Lawrence took a long drink while Thomas kept a careful eye on him. He was walking a tight rope and had no wish to antagonise his master.

Lawrence sat on the bed again.

'You're right,' he said quietly. 'I am a romantic. I can love a woman. I love my wife, but not the way she wants.'

He banged into the bed with his fist.

'Not here.' He looked up as if suddenly aware of Thomas standing silent above him.

'Oh sit down man, for heaven's sake,' he said irritably.

Thomas sat carefully upright in the dressing table chair.

63

'Do you like taking ladies to bed, Thomas? Do you?' Lawrence asked. 'Do you enjoy the sexual act?'

Thomas shrugged. 'Well, I have to admit, I do fancy a bit . . .'

'Fancy a bit . . .' Lawrence echoed nodding.

'Well, I'm only normal in that respect . . .' Thomas went on with difficulty.

'Normal . . .' There was a deep self pity in Lawrence's voice. He got up and his mind seemed to wander on to other things.

'Will you stay with me, Thomas. As my man?' he asked suddenly. The valet was taken by surprise. He tried to prevaricate but Lawrence was determined to pin him down. It suddenly mattered very much to him.

'Either you're with me or against me. Choose.'

'Choose, sir?' Thomas asked nervously, playing for time. Lawrence went right up to him.

'Choose now,' he demanded.

'Well, then . . . in that case. I'm with you . . . naturally,' said Thomas most sincerely.

Lawrence offered his hand. Thomas took it. What else could he do?

CHAPTER FIVE

The confidential report of the Queen's specialist couldn't be questioned. Elizabeth was without doubt pregnant. The news was a bombshell to the Bellamys. Lady Marjorie and Elizabeth stayed in their rooms all day and Richard Bellamy gave up all his parliamentary engagements. There was much speculation in the servants' hall but no one except Rose was near to the truth and she was silent as the grave.

In the evening Richard Bellamy asked his daughter to come down to see him in the morning room. When she presented herself she was meek and cautious and ready for the worst.

'I always thought we had a special relationship of affection and trust, Elizabeth. It seems I was sadly mistaken,' Richard began.

'Why?' she asked.

Richard made a slight annoyed cough.

'When Sir Geoffrey questioned you, you told him a deliberate lie. You said the marriage had not been consummated.'

'That's true,' said Elizabeth. 'It hadn't.'

She had been rehearsing this exact conversation all day and was determined to tell the truth, hoping that her father would understand.

It took some courage but she got through with it.

Her father didn't understand.

'I'm sorry, Elizabeth, I may be simple,' he said in a hurt,

angry voice, which maddened Elizabeth. He was neither sorry nor simple. 'But you are telling me that within a few months of your marriage you took a friend, a mutual friend of both of you, to your bed.'

'Yes,' Elizabeth replied.

'We . . . I am not proud of what I did . . . but . . . well it seemed a sort of solution to our problem at the time.'

'You realise what you've done, don't you?' Richard went on, without forgiveness in his voice, 'you've made it impossible for us to get you divorced from Lawrence.'

His mind was still on practical matters.

'Well not on the grounds we discussed, obviously,' she replied.

'On any grounds.' She was making him angry. 'Your mockery of a marriage must go on. You must face the world as the proud parents of a bastard son.'

'A baby partridge,' Elizabeth suggested irreverently.

'Don't make cheap jokes, Elizabeth,' Richard scolded. 'You disgraced yourself and your mother enough already. You know well enough how these things get about.' Elizabeth had had enough of being shouted at.

'That's your real concern, isn't it?' she replied. 'Your precious name. That's always been your worry, hasn't it, father? Not having a name yourself until you married mother, you're the one who trembles most when it's threatened.'

She looked at her father and was surprised to find how much she despised him.

'In all this mess,' she went on quietly, 'you can't actually bring yourself to think of me, can you? You can't see my humiliation. To find myself pregnant after telling Sir Geoffrey that my husband hadn't ever made love to me. Dear

66

God—you feel wronged, you talk of affection and trust lost between us. What about me? Where's your affection for me when I most need it?'

She ran out of the room. If Richard had answered she wouldn't have listened to him.

Richard Bellamy sat down; all his anger had evaporated and he was overcome by a great sense of having failed.

It was Lady Marjorie who gave her daughter the comfort she needed and restored her sense of security. It was the sort of problem a woman could understand better than a man.

Lady Marjorie also concerned herself with more mundane matters. She sent for Mr Hudson and told him formally that Mrs Kirbridge's marriage had not been successful.

'A source of great sadness to all of us, m'lady,' Mr Hudson was tactful.

'Yes,' Lady Marjorie agreed. 'But we must be practical. The house at Greenwich will be disposed of. Rose has already returned to her duties here. Mrs Fellowes will be given a month's notice.'

'That would leave Mr and Mrs Kirbridge's manservant, m'lady,' the butler suggested.

'Yes,' said Lady Marjorie. 'He has impressed me as a young man of resource and he seems to know a great deal about motor cars. Pearce has asked to be allowed to return to the country as a coachman. I think I shall ask Thomas Watkins to be the chauffeur.'

Mr Hudson coughed.

'I agree that he is a young man of resource and familiar with motor cars,' he replied. 'But I have grave doubts as to his moral character. Forgive me speaking so freely, m'lady.'

Lady Marjorie was surprised and disappointed. She asked the butler to give his reasons.

'He has trifled with Rose's affections,' he explained.

'Well, thank you, Hudson,' she said. 'I shall have to think again.'

Mr Hudson was pleased that she didn't question his judgement. The close understanding between mistress and butler was the rock on which the whole household was built.

At teatime when the servants were all assembled Mr Hudson decided to make an announcement on the subject of the chauffeur to clear the air. 'I would like to make it quite plain,' he said, 'that in the event of Mr Pearce giving up his post as chauffeur here, Mr Thomas Watkins will not be in the running.'

Mrs Bridges was immediately suspicious of a plot.

'Why not?' she demanded indignantly. 'What have you been up to?' She knew very well Mr Hudson's private view of Thomas Watkins. 'If he's not required any more at Greenwich, then he ought to come here. It's only natural.'

'That's what I think,' said Edward very boldly.

Ruby the kitchenmaid repeated, 'It's only natural,' loyally echoing the cook.

'It's not natural and Rose knows why,' Mr Hudson enlarged, looking at Rose.

'I don't, Mr Hudson,' she said blankly.

'I'm sure Rose doesn't want her private affairs aired in public,' Mr Hudson went on mysteriously.

'I'm sure I don't know what you're talking about,' said Rose with a shrug.

'I'm talking about the way Mr Watkins has been playing fast and loose with our Rose's affections,' Mr Hudson announced to the room. 'Part of which I was witness to the other night in this very room.'

Rose suddenly understood. 'I wasn't crying because of him, Mr Hudson,' she exclaimed. 'I was crying cause of Miss Elizabeth and the unkind things she'd been saying. It wasn't Thomas. He was trying to comfort me. He was being nice.'

Mr Hudson was put in a very difficult position and he knew he could expect little mercy from Mrs Bridges.

'So now he can be chauffeur again, if he wants, can't he, Mr Hudson,' she said belligerently.

'It's not as simple as that, Mrs Bridges,' he prevaricated. 'I don't make these appointments, you know.'

'But Lady Marjorie asks you for your opinion on occasions, doesn't she?' Miss Roberts, the lady's maid suggested, knowing that Mr Hudson couldn't deny it.

'What about *this* occasion?' Mrs Bridges asked with more than a hint of menace.

Mr Hudson was forced to retreat.

'I can't think why you should be so keen on him,' he said, 'and in spite of my apparent error, I'm still not convinced of his suitability.'

'Of course he's suitable. You got things a bit mixed up, Mr Hudson,' Mrs Bridges replied, safe in the feeling that she had the whole servants' hall behind her. 'You've done that young man an injustice and if you've got any human decency, which we know you have, you'll put what you done wrong to rights.'

Mr Hudson made a strategic withdrawal to his pantry. There he endured the agony of a soul divided against itself: on the one hand he disliked Thomas Watkins and all his ways and if he reversed his opinion he would certainly lose face all round; on the other hand he had been wrong about Rose and unjust to Watkins. Mr Hudson was a man dedicated to justice.

Later he saw Lady Marjorie and the next day Thomas Watkins was offered and accepted the post of chauffeur at 165 Eaton Place.

Like Mr Hudson but for a very different reason Sir Geoffrey Dillon had been forced by the facts into a change of plan. The prospect of Elizabeth giving birth to an illegitimate baby meant that Lawrence Kirbridge instead of being swept aside into limbo would now have to be taken into very serious consideration and wooed as a friend for he could be a very dangerous enemy. It was a happy chance that he was almost penniless and there had been no marriage settlement. Lawrence was bidden to a family conference at Eaton Place.

The opening of the morning room door revealed Sir Geoffrey Dillon and the three Bellamys.

'Darling,' said Lawrence, going up to Elizabeth and embracing her warmly, 'what wonderful news. I'm to be a father,' and here he turned to Lady Marjorie and Richard, 'and you are to be grandparents. Congratulations.'

Sarah would have admired the bravura of it.

'It's no good Lawrence,' Elizabeth replied. 'I've told them everything.'

'Everything?' Lawrence's eyebrows shot up in mock surprise.

'Everything that is relevant,' said Sir Geoffrey flatly.

'Let me say at once that we feel no personal animosity towards you, Lawrence,' Richard chipped in in his role of bearer of the olive branch. 'These things happen. Nature cannot be overruled.'

'Please believe that, Lawrence dear,' Lady Marjorie added her bit.

'And we've simply asked you here to decide what's best to do. For all our sakes,' said Richard with a friendly smile.

Lawrence was wary of all this cosy cordiality. He feared the Greeks even when they were bearing gifts.

'For obvious reasons, Mr Kirbridge,' said Sir Geoffrey, getting straight to the point, 'you must agree to accept official paternity of the child.'

'For obvious reasons?' Lawrence asked, deliberately obtuse.

'I hardly think you would want the rather sordid facts of the case to be widely known,' said Sir Geoffrey.

'Are they sordid?' Lawrence answered. 'I mean wouldn't it be more sordid to suppress the facts? To live a lie? What do we tell the child? I think Elizabeth and I resolved our own particular difficulty in a mature and reasonable way. Who knows, we might even set a fashion . . . ?'

'I'm afraid we haven't time to listen to your flippant modish theories, Lawrence,' said Richard irritably, and Sir Geoffrey frowned. It was the wrong moment to antagonise the boy. 'Simply give us a straight answer,' Richard went on. 'Will you or will you not accept paternity?'

'And if I do?'

'The marriage would continue in name for the time being,' Sir Geoffrey explained. 'Later we can arrange a judicial separation, on some other grounds.'

'That's neat!' Lawrence admitted. 'And what do we do in the meantime? Go back to Greenwich and grin and bear it? Or am I unexpectedly packed off to foreign parts like Elizabeth's poor unfortunate brother?'

That was exactly what Sir Geoffrey had in mind, together of course with all expenses paid and a reasonable allowance.

Before Lawrence made his decision he asked Elizabeth to talk to him in private. They went into the dining room and sat either side of the long bleak table.

'I can't live with you, Lawrence. I'm sorry.' Elizabeth spoke with difficulty. Lawrence said nothing for a long time. 'Will you go abroad?' she asked at last.

'It seems I must since Southwold money is to provide my steamship ticket—and my future bread and butter.'

Elizabeth felt relieved that at least Lawrence was going to be sensible about it.

'You'll be happier than at Greenwich,' she said.

'Greenwich,' he replied. 'Yes. Since I can't write poetry any more I've taken to flippant epitaphs. Here's one for the plaque on our house:

Lawrence Kirbridge lived here

In married state

From 1908 to 1908.'

There was another long unhappy silence. Lawrence turned and looked out of the window.

'Oh God, I love you,' he said quietly.

In the servants' hall Thomas Watkins was receiving the congratulations of his supporters when Mr Hudson came in with a summons to the morning room.

'What am I wanted for, Mr Hudson?' Thomas asked the butler.

'Better come and find out, hadn't you?' Mr Hudson replied.

He was rather annoyed that he hadn't been told the reason himself.

The sight of Lawrence Kirbridge standing by the morning room fire came as an unpleasant surprise to Thomas. He looked round quickly. Sir Geoffrey Dillon, Mrs Kirbridge and Lady Marjorie were all sitting down.

'Thank goodness you're here,' said Lawrence. 'They're trying to take you away from me, but I've told them they can't. You've pledged yourself to me.'

Thomas moistened his lips and decided it was wiser to stay silent.

'Has Hudson spoken to you about coming to work for us, Thomas?' Lady Marjorie asked.

'Yes, m'lady, he has,' Thomas answered.

'But you haven't accepted?' Lawrence walked over and confronted him. 'Thomas remember. We agreed.'

Thomas said nothing.

'I'm going abroad, Thomas,' Lawrence explained, 'possibly for a long time. I can take you with me. Show you the world. Isn't that what you want. To give yourself more scope! Isn't that what you once told me?'

Thomas remained expressionless.

'What's the good of staying here?' Lawrence pleaded. 'Where will that get you? You'll end up like Hudson. For God's sake man, I'm offering you hope and life.'

'I'm grateful for your offer, sir,' replied Thomas very humbly. 'It's very tempting . . . but . . .'

'But what?' Lawrence barked at him.

'Well, it's always been an ambition of mine to work in a noble household,' Thomas confessed.

'You choose servility.' Lawrence was scornful.

73

'No sir,' Thomas was quick to reply. 'I don't choose it.'

Lawrence looked at him and for a moment it seemed he would hit his valet across the face.

'Go to the devil, Thomas,' he said.

'I've been very happy working for you, sir,' Thomas mumbled.

'Go and roast in hell flames,' Lawrence spat at him. 'I don't want sight or sound of you again.' He walked out of the room and slammed the door.

There was a moment of silence.

'Thank you, Thomas,' Lady Marjorie smiled kindly, 'that will be all.'

That evening as Rose was fussing about laying out her evening clothes, Elizabeth made it up with her. She gave her faithful maid a little brooch which she knew that Rose had always liked very much.

'I've been horrid to you these last few weeks, I know,' she said. 'Please forgive me.' And not for the first time in their long friendship Rose forgave her.

As she lay on her bed in the room that had been hers ever since she could remember Elizabeth was at peace for the first time in months. She lay back and closed her eyes listening to the carol singers approaching down Eaton Place.

In the servants' hall they were eating their supper. The singers outside were singing 'The First Noel'. Mr Hudson frowned as they came to the area and feet could be heard on the steps leading down to the back door.

'Oh those wretched singers,' said the butler. 'They had their pennies only last night.'

He got up angrily and strode towards the back door and

opened it. Outside Thomas Watkins was standing carrying his bag.

'Noel, Noel, Noel, Noel,' he sang. 'Born is the King of Israel.'

Mr Hudson frowned petulantly, he didn't think it was very funny.

Thomas gave him a friendly smile.

'Any room at the inn?' he enquired.

CHAPTER SIX

King Edward the Seventh was old and very portly and had but one more year to live but he still very much enjoyed society and especially the company of beautiful and amusing women. Every year his private secretary prepared a list of people living in London suitable to ask the King to a private dinner party. Early in 1909 this signal honour was bestowed on the Bellamys. As Lady Marjorie was the eldest daughter of an ancient Tory political family and Richard Bellamy had been a minister of the crown under the previous government they both of them were no strangers to the Court and had even been in the Ascot house party when the old Queen was still alive but they were decidedly not one of the King's intimate circle. However Lady Marjorie had come to the monarch's rescue at a garden party at Buckingham Palace when he was beset by a posse of Lancashire mayors and had made him laugh. Afterwards he had remarked to the Spanish ambassador what a charming and beautiful woman Southwold's daughter had become and Sir Francis Knollys had made a note of it at the time. As soon as the Bellamys had expressed their willingness to entertain the King, Sir John Alexander arranged to have lunch with Richard to discuss the guest list and the date. This chain of events could be said to have culminated with Lady Marjorie ringing the morning room bell to summon her butler one fine morning in March.

'I have just received confirmation from Buckingham Palace,' she said, 'that His Majesty will be dining here on Thursday week.'

Mr Hudson concealed the feeling of sudden panic that assailed him and composed his face into a gratified proud expression.

'I understand, m'lady,' he replied.

They discussed such practical questions as the hiring of a suitable extra waiter and the traffic problems that might arise out in the street. It was decided that it would be better to keep the information from the other servants until nearer the time.

'I will talk to Mrs Bridges about the food on Monday,' said Lady Marjorie.

'Very good, m'lady,' Mr Hudson replied and cleared his throat. 'Will . . . will Her Majesty be dining, m'lady?'

'No, Hudson,' Lady Marjorie smiled firmly. 'The Queen does not play bridge. A lady has been invited in her place.'

It was a time honoured formula and the butler knew that Mrs Keppel would be among the guests.

On Sunday evening Mr Hudson finding himself alone with Mrs Bridges could no longer keep the news to himself.

'Big dinner party on Thursday, Mrs Bridges,' he confided. 'Something a bit out of the ordinary.'

Mrs Bridges had an intensely curious nature. 'What's she doing telling you before me?' she asked.

'Her ladyship saw fit to inform me first,' Mr Hudson went on, very cool, 'owing to the special nature of the party. There is to be a distinguished guest.'

'Not . . . not Mr Asquith?'

'No, it's not Mr Asquith,' said the butler with a gratified smile at the success of his riddle.

'Not Mr Balfour. There's nothing special about him. He's always coming here,' mused the cook, dismissing the Conservative leader in a somewhat cavalier fashion.

'No, it is not Mr Balfour, nor the Portuguese ambassador, nor is it Doctor W. G. Grace or Miss Vesta Tilley,' Mr Hudson observed. 'Our guest of honour is to be none other than His Majesty King Edward the Seventh, by the Grace of God Defender of the Faith, Emperor of India and the Dominions beyond the seas.'

'The King!' Mrs Bridges exclaimed and sat down suddenly, struck all of a heap as she explained to Miss Roberts later.

'In person,' Mr Hudson said very confidentially, 'and that's for your ears only for the present.'

He picked up the paper.

'Well bless my soul,' said Mrs Bridges. 'Oh dear me. The King! Dining here. Good gracious me.'

A thousand images were chasing each other through her head.

'Quail,' she said suddenly. 'That's his favorite dish,' and she made off to the dresser and started to search among her recipe books.

'I read that in a magazine,' she muttered to herself. 'I cut it out in case, I know I did.'

'You'd better get in plenty of food,' the butler advised. 'I'm told the old man eats like a horse.'

Mrs Bridges put her hands on her hips.

'That's not respectful,' she said in a shocked voice.

'I respect the institution of monarchy as you well know,'

Mr Hudson replied blandly, 'even if I do have certain reservations about the person of the Sovereign.'

'He's all right,' Mrs Bridges prepared to defend the King to the last ditch. 'A loose liver he may be, but he's popular enough.'

'I'm not referring to the present monarch's character, Mrs Bridges,' the butler continued in his best Sunday preaching manner. 'My quarrel is with the Hanoverian succession. As a Scot I would prefer a Stuart on the throne.'

Mrs Bridges blew out her cheeks at this treason.

'But we must make do with what we have,' Mr Hudson admitted magnanimously.

'Stuff and nonsense,' said Mrs Bridges. 'What would this country have done without Queen Victoria? Eh?'

Mr Hudson refused to be drawn into the larger questions of history.

'I don't believe in discussing a hypothesis,' he replied, dismissing the subject.

'You can call him what you like,' the cook said firmly. 'He's our king and he's coming to dinner on Thursday. God bless him,' she added, so there could be no doubt of her loyalty.

'And I haven't told you,' Mr Hudson warned her, 'so when her ladyship informs you on Monday morning, for mercy's sake, act surprised.'

'Oh, m'lady, what a surprise! Oh, bless my soul,' Mrs Bridges held up her hands and threw up her eyes and altogether overdid it so much that Lady Marjorie thought for one dreadful moment that her cook was going to have a fit.

'Oh dear, I am pleased,' she concluded.

'It is rather exciting, isn't it,' said Lady Marjorie. 'He's very fond of his food so we must give him something to his taste.'

Mrs Bridges produced the recipe she had cut from the magazine.

'Yes, m'lady,' she said. 'I've cut out a recipe from the Ladies Journal for quail, m'lady. Done à la Valencienne. He . . . I mean His Majesty, is very partial to quail—it says so here.'

Lady Marjorie knew that wherever he went the King was given quail and was heartily sick of it, unless it was the famous stuffed variety cooked by Miss Rosa Lewis.

She turned Mrs Bridges' mind to other more suitable ideas such as Baron of Lamb. 'There's no one to touch you with lamb, Mrs Bridges, and you know it,' she said and the cook fidgeted with pleasure. 'And we must have the delicious Medoc sauce with poached salmon.'

'Oh yes,' Mrs Bridges replied, scribbling on her slate. 'Like the French ambassador liked so much.'

After nearly an hour of discussion and the performance of many cunning and diplomatic moves by Lady Marjorie, Mrs Bridges returned happily down to her kitchen with a menu written on her slate that she truly believed was entirely of her own suggestion.

The dinner Lady Marjorie and her cook decided on was as follows:

Caviar au blinis.   Royal Natives.
Consommé de Volaile
Saumon d'Ecosse   Sauce Medoc
Paté de Perdrix
Selle d'Agneau de Lait Persillé

Pommes Frou Frou
Petits Pois de Nice à La Menthe
Sorbet au Champagne
Cigarettes Russes
Pintade Rotie   Salade Coeurs de Laitue
Asperges, Sauce Hollandaise
Gâteau
Buissons d'Ecrivisses
Fruits

For the rest of the week the kitchen was put strictly out of bounds to everyone except Mrs Bridges and Ruby as a succession of errand boys brought victuals of every sort from all the best shops in London. The only exception was made for Mr Ball, the butcher, who brought the baron of lamb in person.

'Best spring lamb from our own grazings in Wiltshire, Mrs Bridges,' Mr Ball explained, as he proudly removed the cloth from the scrubbed wicker basket to reveal the honoured corpse to Mrs Bridges' admiring gaze.

Under Mr Hudson's instructions Edward undertook the gargantuan task of cleaning the great silver dishes and covers and epergnes that had remained in the silver cupboard encased in black tissue paper and tied into their green baize bags since Elizabeth's wedding. Rose attacked all the reception rooms, with brush and broom and cloth and went so far as to insist on washing the chandelier in the drawing room.

Mr Bellamy and Mr Hudson went into secret conclave on the subject of wine. For champagne they chose Moet et Chandon, Dry Imperial (1900); for claret the Latour '74, the pride of the cellar. There was some difference of opinion over the choice of a sweet wine for the dessert, Mr Bellamy favouring the Rhine but Mr Hudson being firm for the Chateau Y'quem '81. Over the port there could be no argument, there were still four bottles left in the cellar of the Croft's '72.

When the great day arrived it took Mr Hudson, with the help of Edward, Rose and the hired waiter, all the afternoon to prepare the dining room.

The largest and finest damask cloth was carefully aligned on the table and then laden with a great mass of glass and silver, epergnes and bonbonnières and many bracketed candelabras with silk shades, the whole linked with ivy, arranged in a series of arabesques.

Rose murmured a litany as she laid the places: 'Spoon for caviare, soup spoon, main course knife, savoury knife, spoon for meringue, dessert spoon.'

It may be noted there was no fish knife; Lady Marjorie believing such things were an abomination and only suitable for the middle classes. At 165 Eaton Place the fish was always eaten with two silver forks.

The hired waiter made the napkins into the shape of a bishop's mitre while Rose put small cards into silver holders before each place. There was no card for the King but it surprised Rose that Mrs Keppel was not sitting next to him.

'Lord Crewe's butler tells me,' Mr Hudson explained, 'that she is often placed opposite the King on informal occasions such as this one, so that if His Majesty becomes bored with his dinner companion, Mrs Keppel can enter the conversation and so to speak restore the situation.'

'Fancy that,' said Rose, gazing at the royal chair. 'Funny

to think that in a few hours from now the King of England's posterior will occupy this very seat!'

Mr Hudson sniffed and looked at Rose over his glasses by lowering his head.

'This is hardly the time for such reflections,' he remarked, to dampen such inappropriate thoughts from Rose's head. 'Not with the flowers still to do in the drawing room and all the final polishing in the hall and on the landings.'

'All right,' said Rose. 'It was only a bit of fun—to steady our nerves.'

'Our nerves are perfectly in order, thank you,' the butler assured her, although he had been jumping up and down like a jack-in-the-box all afternoon and consulting his watch every five minutes.

'I still can't see why I can't wait at table same as I always do,' Rose reflected sadly.

'The King objects to female servants waiting at table,' Mr Hudson explained, not for the first time.

'I think the King's mean.'

'Then you can tell him so,' Mr Hudson retorted tartly. Edward laughed. 'Go on Rose, you tell him he's mean, I dare you.'

'All right, I will,' said Rose defiantly and prancing up to the King's chair gave it a curtsey.

'Your Majesty,' said Rose to the chair, 'I'm Rose, the head house parlourmaid and I think you're mean to object to us female servants waiting at table. I thought you liked to have women around you . . .'

'Rose!' Mr Hudson sounded a note of warning.

'Here,' said Rose, making eyes at the King. 'Would you like me to sit on your knee?'

'Out of that chair at once, my girl,' Mr Hudson commanded and Rose obeyed.

'All right,' she said indignantly. 'I'll ask Mrs Keppel. She's ever such a nice lady and she'll put in a word for us female servants.' She looked across the table to Mrs Keppel's place. 'Eh, Alice!' she called.

'Enough,' exclaimed Mr Hudson. 'Out of here, all of you.' And shooing them out he locked the door.

In the kitchen Mrs Bridges grew warmer and warmer and her temper grew worse and worse and Ruby seemed to be always under her feet. Up in the hall Edward and the hired waiter unrolled the special red carpet down the front steps and into the hall. Although it was barely seven o'clock two policemen were already on duty on the pavement and a small crowd had begun to gather suspecting some untoward entertainment.

For such an experienced public figure and Member of Parliament, Richard Bellamy was at heart a shy man. He didn't particularly shine in society and the prospect of his ruler coming to dine in his house secretly appalled him but for his wife's sake he was prepared to put a brave face on it.

Lady Marjorie appreciated this self sacrifice and as they waited in the hall for the royal arrival she adjusted Richard's tie and smiled at him to give him confidence. The other guests were all safely assembled in the drawing room when at eight twenty-five precisely a noise of clapping and cheering came from the street outside.

Richard nodded to Mr Hudson who stepped forward and opened the front door and the King of England walked in. Lady Marjorie curtsied low, as low as was possible, and

Richard Bellamy inclined his head sharply from the neck in the manner reserved only for royalty.

The long dinner proceeded along its appointed course, calmly and serenely. In the heat and fury of the kitchen Mrs Bridges noted with pleasure a report by Rose on the satisfactory nature of the royal appetite. Otherwise Rose kept a sharp eye and ear on the proceedings in the dining room from her place behind the screen in the serving room; she noted that at the King's end of the table the conversation tended to dwell on outdoor sports such as shooting and racing; she actually heard the King telling Lady Marjorie to back one of his colts called Minoru for the Derby. At the other end of the table where Richard Bellamy held sway over Lady Prudence Fairfax and an old flame of his called Millicent Hartfield, the talk was of the daring new dancer, Isadora Duncan and Mr Barrie's new play 'What Every Woman Knows', while in the middle part peopled by admirals and equerries and their wives there was desultory mention of the earthquake in Calabria and the imprisonment of Mr Bottomley for fraudulent conspiracy.

During the dessert Rose saw that the royal fingers were drumming on the table in a threatening, irritated sort of way; the lady on the King's left, the relict of a colonial governor, was a dreadful old bore. Rose peeped round the screen just in time to see Mrs Keppel lean forward towards the monarch.

'Do forgive the interruption, Lady Wanborough,' she said, 'but I simply must ask the King to settle an argument.'

Rose's heart leapt a beat; it was just like it said in books and gossip papers, just like a fairy tale come true.

By the time the royal party had sat down to play bridge

in the drawing room, Mr Hudson and his minions had nearly cleared the dining room. Edward had collected a souvenir in the shape of the King's half smoked cigar butt and the hired waiter had cleaned up so much of the varied contents of the wine glasses that he could hardly stand. In the kitchen Mrs Bridges was able to sit down for the first time for days and taste a slice of her own excellent gateau, delighted that His Majesty had sent down a personal message in praise of the cooking.

In the scullery Ruby started gamely to wash up the mountain of dirty plates and cutlery. As Edward was coming down the back stairs with a tray of dirty plates the further to add to Ruby's travail the back door bell rang insistently and this was followed by a persistent banging.

'Must be one of them reporters,' said Edward, 'after my exclusive story. "How I served the King of England with two helpings of Baron of Lamb" by Edward Barnes, footman to . . .'

The banging continued.

'Hadn't you better see who it is?' said Rose. Edward went to the servants' hall window and peered out.

'It's a woman in a cloak,' he reported. 'All wrapped up . . . can't see her face. That's where they are cunning, you see . . .'

The bell rang again as Mr Hudson came downstairs.

'It's a woman. She keeps ringing,' Rose explained.

'Come with me, Edward,' the butler directed.

He went to the back door and told Edward to unlock it while he waited to confront the would-be intruder.

The door opened to reveal Sarah, looking very pale and haggard.

'I thought you was never going to open it,' she muttered and nearly fell into Edward's arms.

'Well strike me pink,' said Edward.

Edward and Rose helped Sarah to the easy chair in the servants' hall and Mr Hudson followed with thunder on his brow. Mrs Bridges, attracted by the noise, came in from the kitchen.

'What's she doing here?' she asked suspiciously.

'She's ill,' Rose explained. Whatever else she was, Sarah was clearly in the last stage of pregnancy.

She told them how she had run away from Southwold, borrowed the fare to London and then walked across the park from Paddington all the way to Eaton Place in her tight boots just to be with her old friends again.

'What a night to choose, eh?' she said.

'Well she's not staying in this house, not tonight. Not without her Ladyship's permission,' Mr Hudson announced firmly. Having often been bitten he was twice shy of Sarah's stories. 'We've enough to do without her.'

'Oh please,' Sarah pleaded.

'That's final,' said Mr Hudson.

'I'll be kicked out on the streets and it's ever such a cold night,' she moaned and clutched at her stomach as another spasm of pain came over her. Rose was much affected.

'She's in terrible pain,' she said.

'I think it's starting to come,' Sarah groaned.

'She's putting it on. I know her,' Mrs Bridges nodded wisely. She too had her memories of Sarah's deceits. 'All that agony just to get herself a bed for the night.'

'Fetch a towel, Rosie,' Sarah begged in a weak voice which

87

made Mrs Bridges wonder. She went over and whispered something in Sarah's ear and Sarah whispered back.

Mrs Bridges turned to Mr Hudson.

'Her time is come,' she whispered with ominous certainty. Although she was herself a maiden lady, Mrs Bridges was the acknowledged expert on everything that concerned childbirth.

Thoroughly worried and put out Mr Hudson went upstairs to try to attract his mistress away from the royal presence without the fact being noted. It was altogether too big a problem for him to bear single-handed.

Lady Marjorie rose nobly to the occasion; sweeping down to the servants' hall she took one look at Sarah and asked no more questions. Edward was sent off to get Doctor Foley, Rose to warm some blankets, Mrs Bridges to make tea and Ruby, withdrawn for the moment from the sink, to take up an earthenware hot water bottle to the bed in the empty attic bedroom. Telling the butler to get Sarah upstairs as soon as was possible, Lady Marjorie returned to the drawing room to hold the fort.

But even the best laid plans can go wrong. Just as they had half-carried Sarah to the green baize door leading into the hall the front door bell rang and she had to be hastily withdrawn to the safety of the backstairs.

'Ever so exciting, isn't it?' Sarah whispered. 'Like a game of hide and seek.'

The King chose the same moment to take his leave. As Mr Hudson opened the front door Doctor Foley hurried in nearly bumping into his monarch's ample stomach.

It was after four o'clock in the morning when Rose came

down from the attic into the servants' hall. Ruby had long since gone to bed utterly exhausted, but the others were still there waiting, dozing and drinking tea.

Rose was white as a sheet; she hadn't left Sarah's bedside for over five hours.

'She's all right,' Rose announced quietly to the expectant servants' hall, 'but . . .' She broke off, but her meaning was clear. 'It was a little boy,' she said after a pause, and Mrs Bridges started to sob into her handkerchief.

'Perhaps it was for the best after all.' Afterwards nobody could remember who said it first, Miss Roberts or Mr Hudson.

Rose nursed Sarah day and night and after a few days she gradually began to pick up strength again. One thing haunted her.

'Will I be sent back to Southwold?' she asked Rose every time she came into the room. Rose thought it right to pass the question on to Lady Marjorie, and a few days later Lady Marjorie went up to Sarah's room to answer it.

'Your relationship with my son,' Lady Marjorie explained to Sarah, 'gave you certain rights as my husband and Sir Geoffrey Dillon told you. There is a home for you here in this household as long as you care to stay.'

A wave of relief swept over Sarah, she could hardly believe Lady Marjorie could forgive her.

'You may like to undertake some light work about the house, sewing or mending the linen—just to occupy yourself during the day,' Lady Marjorie went on.

'Thank you, m'lady,' Sarah replied, from the bottom of her heart.

'The problem is,' Lady Marjorie continued, 'where you are to sit and have your meals, where to "put yourself".'

'At the moment I'm neither upstairs or downstairs, am I? What you might call in-between, m'lady,' said Sarah, putting it neatly in a nut shell.

Lady Marjorie took the problem to Mr Hudson who put it to a full assembly of the servants' hall. He himself, as honorary president and judge, naturally maintained a carefully neutral attitude but as in other more august gatherings, opinions differed sharply.

'I think it's a disgrace,' said Miss Roberts. 'Giving house room to that slut!' She had early established herself as Leader of the Opposition.

'Well, it would be a bit awkward,' Edward chipped in, 'after all that's happened.' He was one of those middle-of-the-road people easily persuaded by the latest argument.

'Why should we have to put up with her?' Miss Roberts demanded with a sniff.

'She's got to have her meals somewhere, Miss Roberts,' Mrs Bridges reminded the lady's maid, 'and she certainly can't have them up in the dining room with them.'

Mrs Bridges and Rose, sitting by the fire, formed a solid pro-Sarah lobby.

'It won't be you taking her tray up neither,' Rose threw across the room at Miss Roberts who was sitting flanked by Ruby and Edward and the long dining table.

'Well I think . . .' said Ruby suddenly.

'We don't want to know what you think, Ruby,' Mrs Bridges cut in firmly, exercising the dictatorship of the kitchen.

'After all she's done and the shame she's brought on us,' Miss Roberts enlarged her theme.

'What shame's she brought on you Miss Roberts?' Rose demanded putting the lady's maid out of her stride.

'She's a stuck up lying minx,' Miss Roberts spluttered, refusing to be silenced. 'Thinks she's better than any of us, putting on airs, gets poor Captain James into such trouble he has to be sent off to India and then thinks she can just walk in here.'

'We're none of us perfect,' Mrs Bridges broke in tartly. 'Not even you Miss Roberts.'

The two elderly ladies regarded each other across the table like two old jealous tabby cats fighting over a piece of fish.

'I'll see she behaves herself this time. Have a heart, Miss Roberts,' Rose conciliated. 'How would you like to be . . .'

'I wouldn't ever be in such a disgusting position,' Miss Roberts broke in, 'in anyone's house.'

'I'll bet!' Edward remarked to the company in general.

'How dare you speak to me like that!'

Mr Hudson, seeing the discussion developing into a slanging match, decided it was the moment to call upon the voice of reason.

'I put it to you all,' he began holding his lapels in his best legal manner, 'that Sarah, for all her faults and for all the troubles and upsets she has brought upon this noble house, is nonetheless capable of better things. She is an able seamstress and she is possessed of a cheerful disposition.

'Unfortunately,' he went on, 'as a maid here she developed ideas well above her station and fell from grace.'

He paused and looked round in a manner reminiscent of the late Mr Gladstone.

'Sarah has paid a bitter price,' he reminded them. 'She has lost her child. She is beaten.'

Mrs Bridges began to make ominous use of her handkerchief.

'If the Master and Her Ladyship can see the way to exercising tolerance and kindness and forgiveness towards this unfortunate girl, then who are we . . . as Christians . . . to deny this young person ours?'

It was a powerful human argument powerfully put and Miss Roberts knew she was beaten. She rose.

'All right,' she said defiantly. 'Let the wretched girl have her meals here—as long as I don't have to sit next to her.'

Almost before Mr Hudson had reached the drawing room to inform Lady Marjorie of their decision, Rose had reached Sarah's bedroom taking the last flight of stairs two at a time in a most unprofessional manner.

'It will be just like old times,' Rose exclaimed happily. 'We'll have some laughs again, eh Sarah?'

Sarah nodded, too overcome to reply.

'But you've got to promise me one thing mind,' Rose went on, sounding a well known note of caution.

'I've got to behave myself, haven't I?' Sarah said in a humble contrite voice.

'You really have got to this time, Sarah,' Rose answered. 'I'm serious.'

'Ooh I will, Rosie,' Sarah promised. 'Honest!'

And she really meant it. Which only goes to prove that human nature is capable of almost endless self deception.

CHAPTER SEVEN

Thomas Watkins found he had his work cut out to get the garage in the mews at the back of 165 Eaton Place into some sort of order. Mr Pearce had done very little to alter the old stables to suit the requirements of the motor car.

Thomas set about removing the signs of a hundred years of occupation by the horse. He painted the whole place from top to bottom, converted the tack room into a mechanic's workshop and made a work-bench from the long table that had once served as a brushing bench for the horse rugs.

All was ready for a new motor car. Some might think it fickle of Thomas to have fallen out of love with the Renault so soon, but he had set his mind on having a Rolls Royce. Every time he took the Bellamys to a ball or a large dinner party or a reception he had ample time to contemplate with envy the other chauffeurs who had in their charge these large and elegant machines made by the new British company in Derby.

One day Thomas mentioned to his new master the excellence of the latest Rolls Royce model, the Silver Ghost, and touched on the advantages both social and political that would accrue to the owner of such a fine piece of British machinery. Mr Bellamy took the point; in his constituency it would be better to be seen driving a British rather than a foreign made motor car. Lady Marjorie had noted with pleasure how smart the new chauffeur looked in his uniform and applauded the many improvements in the garage department so that she readily agreed to Thomas' suggestion. The motor car was expensive, nearly one thousand four hundred pounds, but then as Thomas pointed out, it was an investment in itself.

It was a proud day when Thomas manoeuvred the great car down the mews and through the double doors into the garage. It had six cylinders and the power of forty-five horses at a thousand revolutions and a straight cut gear system with three gears and a reverse. The bonnet was of polished steel and the Roi de Belges body was by Barker's and painted a warm grey.

The passenger compartment was very roomy and tall enough to accommodate a gentleman still wearing his top hat. All the woodwork inside was polished mahogany and there was a shelf that opened out to make a table and revealed a complete set of cut glass decanters with silver tops. A brass speaking tube led from this compartment to behind the driver's seat for ease of communication.

The new car was so long and so high that it nearly filled the whole garage.

To celebrate his elevation to the superior position of chauffeur from the common rank of manservant Thomas had grown a moustache; and one morning while he was brushing this new and happily luxuriant growth with a small brush especially made for the purpose and was savouring the pleasant sharp smell of oil and metal which reminded him of his family's bicycle shop in South Wales, he was disturbed by the arrival of Sarah in the garage.

He had been aware of the disturbances caused by her dramatic re-entry into the Bellamy household and had been intrigued enough by Edward's description of Sarah's chequered history as well as by the bright eyes and increasingly trim figure of this pale and interesting new arrival, to make a mental note that when times were more propitious a more intimate acquaintance with the young lady in question might be to his advantage.

Sarah was carrying a small bouquet of carnations garnished with fern.

'Well Sarah,' said Thomas, 'there's a kind thought. A nice button-hole is it?'

'It's not for you, Mr Watkins, it's for the car,' Sarah explained pertly.

Any embellishment for his motor car pleased Thomas Watkins so he helped by filling the little trumpet-shaped flower vase that fitted into a holder in the passenger compartment.

Sarah sat herself down on the back seat and looked round in admiration.

'It's like a little room, isn't it?' she remarked. 'You could live quite comfy in here, couldn't you?'

'Never been in a motor car before?' Thomas asked, handing her the vase. Sarah shook her head.

'Tell you what, why don't I take you for a little spin?' he suggested. 'When I fill her up with petrol.'

Sarah didn't seem to hear him. She picked up the speaking tube and he went into the driver's seat to show her how it worked.

'Go on say something,' he said.

'Wilkins, you stoopid fellow,' said Sarah, in a very grand imitation of Lady Marjorie's voice. 'Watch out, my man, you nearly hit that horse. Are you intoxicated?'

Thomas swung the wheel over sharply.

'I'm teetotal, m'lady,' he explained. 'Must be the springtime in my blood.'

'Don't answer me back fellow, or I shall be obliged to discharge you without a character.'

She started to unpin the antimacassars from the backs of the seats. They were to be taken over to the house to be washed.

'When's your day off then?' Thomas asked her. 'Hampstead Heath's very nice this time of the year.'

If Sarah was pleased at the chauffeur's interest in her she didn't show it.

'Mr Watkins, you forget yourself,' she retorted, as she flounced away. 'I am no longer a domestic servant, while *you*' and here she gave him a look of utter disdain, 'you are still a mere "shover".'

Thomas shook his head as he turned back to his work. She had a bit of spirit had Sarah.

Sarah had also been impressed.

'He's got a funny way of putting things, that Thomas,' she said to Rose as they ironed the antimacassars. 'Makes you laugh, doesn't he?'

'Very comical,' Rose replied without enthusiasm. In the larger servants' hall society she had seen very little of Thomas Watkins and she missed his company more than she would have liked to admit. 'Now don't you let him put his dirty fingers on that lace.'

'I thought you liked him,' said Sarah probing.

'Thomas,' Rose replied in her most non-committal voice. 'He's very clever at getting the right side of people, is Thomas Watkins, especially ladies. I know him,' she warned, folding the clean antimacassars and wrapping them in a clean cloth.

'All talk and compliments and that, but all the time he's got his eye on the next step, looking ahead like over your shoulder. He'll flirt with you as long as you're useful to him.' She turned to her sheets again. 'You just watch out, Sarah . . . and don't keep going over there wasting his time and yours.'

As she went out Sarah wondered if it really would be a waste of time. She would just have to see.

When the garage doors were open and Thomas was cleaning the gleaming steel of the Rolls' bonnet in the sunlight it attracted the admiration of many passers-by in the mews who would stop for a chat with the chauffeur.

That morning was no exception, the admirer in question being a seedy middle-aged Irishman wearing a shapeless tweed suit and sporting a rather battered bowler. In the manner of such persons he was fond of the sound of his own voice and before many minutes were over he was telling Thomas the tale of how he had been a soldier fighting on the North West Frontier of India in the Khyber Rifles.

'I was batman to Captain Hammond,' said the Irishman. 'Captain Charles Hammond,' he added with point.

Thomas glanced round at the man feeling a twinge of sorrow for Captain Hammond.

'Friend of your Lady Bellamy's,' the Irishman added and Thomas realised that the man wasn't just in the mews to admire the motor car.

The Irishman described how he had been repulsed from the front door of 165 Eaton Place by Mr Hudson. 'Treated me like I was a tinker or suchlike,' he complained, 'and me an ex-serviceman . . . If there's one class of person I can't be doing with it's butlers.' Thomas reflected that at least they had that in common. 'I only wanted a word with her ladyship,' the man went on, beginning to whine a little. 'I was only thinking she'd like to have her property back, that's all . . .'

'Her letters . . .' Thomas continued to polish the bonnet.

'And other items,' the Irishman lowered his voice. 'An opery programme, a lace handkerchief, a photygraph of her ladyship. Mementoes you might say. They meant a lot to the Captain, kept them in his tin box he did along with his decorations.'

Thomas decided that the more secluded atmosphere of his workshop was more suitable for such confidential information. Over a cup of tea brewed on Thomas' gas ring, the Irishman, whose name was Dooley, told the sad brave tale of Captain Hammond's death, killed instantly by an Afridi spear through his liver with the same Dooley fighting gallantly by his side.

On going through his master's effects Dooley had come upon the letters and rather than let them fall into the hands of the authorities with the rest of the Captain's kit he had come on a sort of pilgrimage with them all the way back to England just so that the Captain's old widowed mother who lived in Cheltenham shouldn't ever discover the shocking fact that her son had been canoodling with a married woman before his death.

'And the wife of a Tory M.P. at that,' Dooley added. 'Do you follow me?'

Thomas followed him very well but concealed any interest he might have in the matter.

'You know what you should do with those letters,' he advised. 'Burn them. To ashes.'

'Women can be very sentimental about such things,' the Irishman countered. 'It occurred to me her Ladyship would like them back.'

'I'll tell you what,' Thomas proposed brightly. 'You give them to me and I'll see she gets them.'

Mr Dooley made it clear that he was disappointed in Thomas' reaction to his confidences. He had been hoping to find a more intelligent listener ready to share the reward with him on equal terms.

'What kind of reward were you looking for?' Thomas asked. Dooley looked at the chauffeur and at the car wondering how high he could pitch it. No doubt the Bellamys were people of some wealth.

'About a hundred pounds, shall we say,' he suggested.

Thomas was scornful. A hundred pounds was a ridiculous price for a bunch of letters whatever they contained, even if they existed.

Dooley had a sample of his wares with him and the page of the letter Thomas was privileged to read left him in no doubt that it was very genuine indeed. He told the Irishman to come back the next day.

In the manner of any good detective Thomas needed to double check the evidence. He needed further proof of Lady Marjorie's infidelity and he knew that if it existed he would be able to get it from the other servants. He decided to try Sarah out as a go-between. She knew nothing of the business herself not being employed at 165 at the time but she could find out about it from Rose. That afternoon in the linen room by offering Rose some confidential tidbits of her own love affair with James Bellamy she lured the older maid into telling her the torrid tale of Lady Marjorie's Moment of Madness, as Rose put it, three summers before.

'Did the Master know about it?' Sarah enquired.

'Course not, silly, but we all did downstairs.'

By that evening, Thomas was in command of all the facts he needed.

The chauffeur pondered long and hard on the delicate subject of Captain Hammond's letters and the next day when he was driving through Hyde Park he stopped the motor car in a secluded spot.

'Begging your pardon, m'lady, I have something most important to say to you,' he began speaking through the tube but realising the impossibility of conducting a long and difficult conversation by that means began to wind down the window connecting the driver with the passenger compartment.

'What are you doing?' Lady Marjorie demanded in amazement. 'Wind up that window immediately and take me to Bond Street.'

It took Watkins all his native wit to convince his mistress that she was indeed being blackmailed.

'You say this . . . this batman is asking for money in exchange for the letters?' Lady Marjorie asked at last.

'I'm afraid so, m'lady,' Thomas admitted unhappily. 'I thought you'd like to know what the position was m'lady. I hope you don't mind me mentioning it.'

'No Thomas,' said Lady Marjorie almost gratefully. 'You did quite right. I think perhaps you'd better not mention this man to anyone else.'

'Oh no, m'lady,' Thomas agreed in a shocked voice. Nothing Lady Marjorie could have said could have more surely convinced her chauffeur of the value of the letters.

'What . . . er . . . reward is the man asking, Watkins?' she demanded.

'Er . . . two hundred pounds.'

He hadn't meant to say 'two' but it just slipped out. He took a quick look at Lady Marjorie's face in the driving mirror to see how she had taken it. Better than he had expected.

'That's a great deal of money,' she said.

'That's what I told him,' Thomas replied, keen to show whose side he was on.

A quick decision by Lady Marjorie's paternal great grandfather had saved his regiment at Badajoz and she had inherited this family gift for decisiveness, but in this case she was put in a quandary. She had to raise two hundred pounds quickly. If she used the bank her husband would know of it and question her. She looked at Watkins. He was a young man of resource.

'Tell me,' she asked, 'are there not establishments where it is possible to raise a loan? On security of some possession?'

Thomas twisted round. In Lady Marjorie's hand was a small jewel case and in it a pearl necklace that she had been taking to the jewellers to have restrung.

'I understand, m'lady,' Thomas said quietly. He knew just the place kept by a Jew from Swansea down the Fulham Road.

When Dooley called that night Thomas was just changing his clothes in his bedroom above the garage. It was a large, bleak room and Thomas cared little for its arrangements, his heart being below. He heard Dooley in the garage and called him up and offered him a glass of beer.

'You're lucky to catch me,' Thomas remarked. 'I was just going over to the house for my supper.'

'Had a word with her ladyship?'

'Yes I have,' Thomas replied, very flat and without enthusiasm.

'I'll wager it was quite a shock for her, poor soul,' said the Irishman with something like glee in his voice, 'finding her little indiscretion come to light. Thought she'd got away with it, did she?'

'No, I don't think that's what she thought,' Thomas was very busy with his collar. Dooley frowned.

'It wasn't such a dark and guilty secret as you imagined, see?' said Thomas.

Dooley was indignant.

'Well it ought to be,' he said. 'A married woman, carrying on like that and her in high society.'

'Oh, they don't pay a great deal of attention to these things in High Society. Not nowadays,' Thomas assured his visitor as he concentrated on the exact adjustment of his tie. 'No,' he went on, 'Mr Bellamy knows all about the letters. I'm afraid you've been under a grave misapprehension.'

He began to pomade and brush his moustache with elaborate care.

'Well I've never heard anything like it in my life,' the Irishman exclaimed in a shocked voice. 'Condoning, that's what it is. Condoning his wife's adultery. And him a Member of Parliament. Holy Mother of God, what are we coming to?'

Thomas went over to put on his coat and waistcoat.

'We're coming to the point, Mickey,' he said casually, 'where we can admit those letters are a lot of useless rubbish.' He put on his waistcoat. 'Oh Lady Marjorie said she'd give you a fiver for them; she'd like the photograph,' he went on, as if he just remembered it. 'Only in the way of charity.'

Dooley was almost overwhelmed with righteous indignation.

'Upper crust,' he fumed, 'I wouldn't give you tuppence for the lot of them.'

'Never mind the tuppence, do you want the fiver?' Thomas produced a crisp new five pound note from his pocket as if by magic and held it up in front of the Irishman's nose.

It seemed for a moment that Thomas was to be an easy victor but Mr Dooley was made of sterner stuff and had been brought up on this sort of contest with his mother's milk.

He looked sad and hurt.

'A man in my position,' Dooley avowed, 'a good Christian like meself mind, maybe has a duty to expose the immoral behaviour of those in high places. Maybe the public has a right to know how their betters behave themselves in the privacy of their wealthy homes.'

Thomas pretended to be unimpressed.

'I don't see it's their business, really,' he said loftily. 'Not the ordinary common herd.'

'And who elected Mr Bellamy to the Parliament, will you tell me that?' Dooley demanded, warming to his work. 'The ordinary honest working-man that's who put him up there in Westminster.'

And he proceeded to go off into a colourful diatribe on the baseness and immorality of the ruling classes finishing up by declaring that he would give Lord Northcliffe the letters and the whole story and get himself well paid for his trouble at the same time.

Thomas didn't like the talk about Lord Northcliffe and his newspapers in the least but he saw himself losing out all round and getting the sack and no reference into the bargain.

'All right,' he agreed rather hastily. 'I'll pay you the hundred pounds—on her ladyship's behalf.'

Thomas realised his error as soon as the words were out of his lips. You couldn't get away with a mistake like that with a man like Dooley.

'So you've got the money after all,' the Irishman almost hooted. 'Call my bluff, would you, you bloody lying Welshman.'

'Take the money and be gone,' Thomas said sharply.

'I'll not be ordered about by a lying Taffy,' Dooley continued. 'It'll cost you another hundred now, to pay you out for your deceit and you can tell the lady why. Two hundred pounds it is. By tomorrow night.'

Thomas went to bed that night smarting under his defeat. He certainly wasn't going to let the Dooley have the two hundred pounds—he would have no pride and no money left. Gradually a plan began to form in his mind. It was a bold plan relying on his judgement of Mr Bellamy's character; but Thomas liked a risk and if it succeeded it would salve his damaged honour for a very adequate return.

The next day when Lady Marjorie had gone out and Mr Bellamy was working in the morning room, Thomas went to see Mr Hudson in his pantry saying that he felt it was his duty to ask the butler's advice on a certain confidential matter. Mr Hudson listened to the tale of Mr Dooley, pleased that Thomas was showing some sense of propriety at last.

'You were right to come to me,' Mr Hudson told him. 'London is full of such people, Mr Watkins, confidence tricksters no less.'

'Oh. Well I'm glad there's no truth in what Mr Dooley says, Mr Hudson,' Thomas answered innocently, and went back to his garage and waited anxiously. Within half an hour he was relieved to get the expected message that the Master would like to speak to him in the morning room.

Within minutes he was standing in front of Richard Bellamy in a respectful manner, head down, cap in hand.

'In the ordinary way I'd have no compunction in handing this man over to the police, but since my wife's honour is apparently being challenged I intend to proceed more delicately,' Mr Bellamy explained carefully. 'You understand what I mean, don't you, Watkins?'

'Oh yes, indeed, sir?' Thomas replied; he knew very well what Mr Bellamy meant and was greatly relieved that his plan was working so well.

'I do not intend to allow her ladyship to be in any way upset,' Mr Bellamy went on.

'Oh no, sir!' the chauffeur was in vehement agreement once again.

'You haven't of course said anything to her about this man?'

Thomas flushed at the suggestion.

'How could you think I'd do a thing like that, sir?' he asked reproachfully.

Mr Bellamy coughed, rather ashamed of himself.

'Well since you have shown such excellent discretion so far may I rely on your discretion a little further?'

By luncheon Thomas had another two hundred pounds to join the first two hundred in his little cardboard attaché case under his bed.

After dinner in the servants' hall Sarah went over to the garage at Thomas' bidding. Together they had a long conversation.

By six o'clock when Dooley came back, Thomas was ready for him.

'The price has been agreed,' he told Dooley. The Irishman was pleased but at the same time unhappy he had not asked for more.

'Let's see the colour of your money,' he demanded, still suspicious of a trick.

Thomas looked at him in surprise.

'Do you expect my mistress, a lady of quality, to trust me, a simple chauffeur, a mere servant, with two hundred pounds in bank notes.'

'I wouldn't trust you with a baby's rattle myself,' the Irishman admitted quite frankly.

'There you are then,' Thomas replied not allowing himself to punch Mr Dooley in the teeth as he would have wished. 'Her Ladyship wishes to receive the letters back from you personally.'

There was a gleam of interest in the Irishman's eyes as Thomas explained to him the plan. He was to come back to the garage later that evening when Lady Marjorie would be waiting for him sitting in the back of the car on her return from a bridge party.

'You know I like the idea,' Dooley said smiling and shaking his head at the thought of meeting Lady Marjorie in such romantic circumstances. 'I like it very much . . .'

When the headlights of the big car lit up the garage as it turned in from the mews shortly after ten thirty that night Dooley was waiting. Thomas climbed out and escorted the Irishman to the passenger's door. It was dark but Dooley could see the dark outline of a lady in the car, veiled and mysterious just as he expected.

'Private Michael Dooley, m'lady,' Thomas announced in a formal voice and ushered Dooley into the car. He sat gingerly on the seat next to Lady Marjorie, so close that he could smell her fine perfume.

'It's very kind of your ladyship to receive me personally, in your motor car,' Dooley began politely.

'There was little alternative since I am not accustomed to receive common soldiers in my drawing room,' came the haughty reply.

Sarah had been practising her Lady Marjorie accent all the afternoon.

'I may be a common soldier but I've got a living to earn,' said Dooley, a trifle indignant. 'Times are very hard, you know, I've not got enough put by to feed a cat. Seven years serving His Majesty and not even a gratuity.'

'So you resort to blackmail.'

'There's no need to be insulting,' Dooley sounded hurt. 'A woman in your position shouldn't behave like that. It isn't right.' Dooley sniffed. 'Don't you want ordinary people to respect you?'

'Not particularly, Mr Dooley.' The voice was so withering that Dooley knew it must truly be a lady of quality beside him.

'Well now what about the money your ladyship,' Dooley suggested. But the lady was suspicious and called on her chauffeur.

'Can we trust this fellow, Wilkins?' she asked.

Thomas popped his head through the window.

'Up to you, m'lady,' he said.

'How do I know you were a friend of Captain Hammond's?' she asked.

'I was his batman, wasn't I?' Dooley replied indignantly.

'I can prove it. He had a mole on his left wrist. You'd remember that,' he added pointedly.

'Ah yes!' said Sarah with a tragic sigh. 'I do remember. Poor Charles and his mole.'

Thomas had a suspicion that Sarah had a tendency to overact.

'Begging your pardon, m'lady,' he said. 'I think we'd better get on with the business.'

'Not till Mr Dooley has heard what I think of him,' she said to Thomas, turning away so that the Irishman couldn't see and putting out her tongue.

She turned back to Dooley, raised her lorgnettes and gave him a look of fierce disdain.

'Aren't you ashamed to batten on a woman's frailty?' she demanded. 'Unprincipled wretch! Villain! Stinking blackguard!'

Dooley recoiled and Thomas cast his eyes up to heaven in silent supplication.

'The transaction, m'lady,' he almost shouted in her ear. To calm him down they offered Dooley some whisky in a cut glass tumbler poured from one of the beautiful decanters. 'Your health, m'lady,' he said and downed the lot at a gulp.

'I'll take the money,' said Thomas, taking something from Sarah.

'Then you can hand over the letters, Mr Dooley,' said Sarah. The Irishman produced a packet from his pocket tied with pink string.

'Do you recognise them, m'lady?' he asked.

'Indubitably,' Sarah replied and wiped away a tear. 'The sight upsets me a little. Wilkins give him the money and let us end this painful ceremony.'

As Dooley leant forward eagerly to take the money from Thomas, Sarah swung her bag and brought it down with a thump on the back of his head. Dooley collapsed into the chauffeur's arms.

Sarah jumped out of the car.

'I ain't killed him, have I?'

'Just about,' said Thomas. 'What's in that bag?'

'Only half a brick,' she admitted.

But Dooley was breathing steadily and when they had poured the rest of the whisky over him and collected the letters and the money Thomas frogmarched him into the mews.

'Come along my old wounded soldier,' he said in a friendly way. 'Left, right . . . left, right. I'm going to dump you in the gutter where you belong.'

As luck would have it they bumped into a police constable in Eaton Square and Thomas was able to explain that he had found the Irishman lying in the road.

As the strong arm of the law propelled the half conscious Dooley in the direction of Gerald Row police station Thomas reflected with some satisfaction that it was the last he was likely to see of his Irish friend.

Sarah was waiting for Thomas up in his bedroom with the letters.

'I think you're very clever, Wilkins,' she said in her Lady Marjorie voice. He went over to her and kissed her.

'You didn't do so bad yourself, love,' he replied putting the money back into the suitcase. Sarah was watching him closely.

'There's more than two hundred quid in there,' she said suspiciously.

'There's four hundred.' He hadn't told her the whole truth

before. Sarah was shocked at his obvious intention to keep the lot.

'A man's entitled to a fee for handling such delicate negotiations,' he explained. Sarah didn't agree. She couldn't believe that he would do anything so underhand and dishonest to such good employers. It made him no better than Mr Dooley.

'If you're going to do something and get sacked, you might as well do something really big,' she said with reason. Thomas had never before considered that the reward of virtue could in the long run be more valuable than much fine gold and it gave him much food for thought and at the same time increased his respect for Sarah. All night long his devious mind wrestled with plan after plan; in every one there was the same snag. There was only one package of letters but two people had paid for them. After dawn the simple solution occurred to him. He would divide them.

As soon as Lady Marjorie had left the house Thomas sought an audience with his master and handed him half the letters tied in red ribbon together with the two hundred pounds.

'I'd like to show that I appreciate your honesty,' said Mr Bellamy as he set a match to the letters in the morning room grate. 'Some servants in your position, entrusted with two hundred pounds would have made up some cock and bull story and pocketed the lot.'

'Well you see, sir,' Thomas replied piously, 'I was brought up very strict, my father being an elder in the chapel.'

To be truthful, Mr Watkins senior hadn't seen the inside of a chapel for thirty years and if there was any God he worshipped it was Bacchus.

'Quite,' said Mr Bellamy, taking two five pound notes from the pile of money. 'I am going to give you ten pounds to spend in any way you choose.'

'I'm very grateful, sir,' the chauffeur replied from the bottom of his heart.

In the afternoon Thomas drove Lady Marjorie into the park and returned her two hundred pounds.

'You are wonderfully discreet, Watkins,' she said. 'I shall give you a small reward for your trouble. I believe the usual thing for the return of stolen property is ten per cent.'

She had almost to force him to accept the twenty pounds and afterwards they visited the pawnshop in Fulham and redeemed Lady Marjorie's necklace.

After supper Mr Hudson took Thomas aside.

'So it's all cleared up, is it, the matter of the Irishman and the letters?' he enquired confidentially.

'Oh that matter,' Thomas answered in guarded tones. 'Yes, I think so, Mr Hudson. He's not been back to the mews again.'

'In other words, the whole affair was indeed a shocking attempt to extort money from her ladyship for some non-existent letters—as I forecast,' said the butler smugly.

'Quite, Mr Hudson,' Thomas agreed. Who was he to contradict such a great person as the butler?

Sarah was quite indignant when Thomas told her that he had given all the money back.

'What and not made nothing out of it,' she asked. 'Not even a bob or two? That's not right, after all you've done.'

'Oh I've made something,' Thomas assured her. 'Not much and I didn't ask for it. Here's your share.'

He gave her three pounds and Sarah was delighted.

'They both trusted you and you didn't let them down,' she said happily, putting the notes to her cheek.

'Did you think I would?' he asked her with a smile.

'Well,' said Sarah. 'I'd like to think I'd made an honest man out of you, Mr Wilkins.'

'Watkins,' said Thomas, pushing Sarah onto the bed and kissing her.

'He's a good man, I've changed my opinion of him lately,' said Richard Bellamy. He and his wife were discussing the chauffeur over coffee that evening.

'A good chauffeur. Smooth and reliable,' he added, with a nod.

'Safe and trustworthy,' Lady Marjorie chimed in. 'Do you think we could increase his wages a little?'

'I've already done so,' said her husband as he handed her his cup to be refilled.

CHAPTER EIGHT

In May the house was invaded by an army of workmen come to redecorate the nurseries in preparation for Elizabeth's baby and to install a new electric bell system. Lady Marjorie took Elizabeth down to Southwold to be out of the way and she took Thomas and the Rolls Royce motor car with her and Rose to act as the lady's maid and see her relations, leaving Miss Roberts to go through her boudoir and all her clothes in preparation for the summer season. Sarah was sent off to be trained as a nurserymaid. Elizabeth knew that she would have to accept old Nanny Webster in charge but she thought that if Sarah knew the modern methods which she herself favoured she would at least have an ally when the baby arrived. For the time being Thomas and Sarah's blossoming friendship was brought to a standstill.

The continual banging and hammering throughout the house and the plaster dust that seemed to penetrate every nook and cranny soon began to get on everyone's nerves upstairs and downstairs. Upstairs Richard Bellamy found it difficult to concentrate on his work and grew irritable with the butler who in turn took it out on all and sundry below stairs. The same morning that Mr Hudson received a telegram and Mr Bellamy's brother Arthur rang up to ask to stay, a black cat crossed the servants' hall threshold.

'There's going to be trouble and that's for sure,' said Mrs Bridges, who believed in omens. Edward was inclined to agree with her; he had seen Mr Hudson's face when he had read the telegram and had watched through the keyhole afterwards as Mr Hudson took relief in a strong dram of whisky. And as if that wasn't enough to indicate that something was wrong Mr Hudson continued the morning in a filthy temper and found fault with everyone.

Violet the new underhouse parlourmaid had been idle about her dusting; Miss Roberts had carelessly dropped one of Lady Marjorie's gloves on the stairs; Ruby was chopping parsley in the servants' hall because the kitchen was too full of grit and dust and Edward who had been caught once already smoking his abominable new pipe and reading the *Sporting Life* was laying up the two trays for luncheon with dirty tray cloths. It should be explained that owing to the workmen the dining room was shut and the Bellamy brothers were to eat their meals off trays in the morning room.

'That tray cloth is soiled,' Mr Hudson said testily, pointing at the offending stain.

'The plate'll cover it, Mr Hudson,' Edward explained.

'It's for Mr Arthur Bellamy, the Master's brother. Fetch a clean cloth at once.'

'Mr Arthur? He's not anyone, he's a doctor,' Edward replied unwisely.

'Respect is not something which we grade according to title or to wealth, Edward,' Mr Hudson pontificated. 'It is a matter for us, of what is owed by servant to master. And a brother, in any walk of life, is someone to whom much is owed; the greatest consideration, the greatest formality, no matter how the exigencies of fortune have led each into different paths and to different fortunes.'

Mr Hudson deliberately overturned the tray onto the table.

'Now do as you're told,' he commanded. Edward gave a shrug. He concluded that something in that telegram had really got Mr Hudson's goat.

Mr Arthur Bellamy arrived at a quarter past twelve. Hudson relieved him of his coat and gloves and his bowler hat. As Arthur moved towards the morning room door the butler had to hurry to precede him.

'I will announce you, sir,' he said.

'Announce me to my own brother,' Arthur Bellamy replied testily.

'It is customary, sir, in this house.'

Arthur shrugged helplessly.

'Well if it amuses you,' he said.

Arthur Bellamy was Richard's elder brother and was truly as it is so often said the reverse of the coin. Whereas Richard was handsome and well mannered and a gentleman of liberal persuasions his brother was short and ill formed, inclined to be offhand and arrogant and self opinionated. They had never liked each other.

'Mr Arthur Bellamy, sir,' Mr Hudson announced.

'Arthur, my dear fellow.'

'Well I'm here,' said Arthur, 'greeted at the door by two flunkeys.'

'As you should be,' Richard was conciliatory.

'One smelling of whisky,' said Arthur, satisfied at his brother's look of amazement. 'The Scots always drink whisky, don't they?'

Richard Bellamy was used to his brother's bad moods; he had had to endure them off and on all his life. That morning Arthur Bellamy had failed to be elected a member of the

Royal Society and was bitterly hurt by it. Richard let him grizzle on until Edward came in with their luncheon.

Downstairs Mr Hudson was late for servants' hall dinner. It was most unusual and Mrs Bridges put it down to the black cat. Edward blamed it on the telegram and found support from Ruby.

'Perhaps his mother's been took sick,' she suggested. It was something she could understand, her own mother having a weak constitution.

'Mr Hudson's mother passed on two years come Easter, Ruby,' Mrs Bridges said, putting the girl in her place. 'Now you just go and bring in the stew while it's hot, and mind you don't drop it.'

In the library the two Bellamy brothers were eating baked gammon and parsley sauce.

'You'd hardly know the old village,' Arthur remarked. 'Ugly new buildings on the outskirts, motor cars filling the air with dust and fumes, strangers everywhere. Of course you never come down to witness it.'

'It's hard to find time,' Richard admitted.

'I do understand,' Arthur replied in a bitter voice and taking up his napkin put it to his face with a grimace of distaste.

'There's grit in the parsley sauce,' he said. Richard had to admit there was a hint of it.

'You're taken advantage of,' said Arthur. 'It's not surprising. The servant classes have a nose for social weaknesses.'

'I think they are loyal, Arthur,' Richard replied.

'Really,' Arthur was clearly sceptical. 'When your wife is at home is there grit in the parsley sauce?'

Richard Bellamy shrugged at the pettiness of his brother's remark.

'Unwashed vegetables are the cause of much disease, both physical and mental,' Arthur continued, pushing his plate forward. 'At home, Anthea washes all such foods in chlorinated water. It is a humble abode but we have our standards.'

'Humble abode,' his brother retorted. 'Fifteen rooms and two acres of land and you live in extreme comfort.'

'You can't eat this,' said Arthur. 'It must be sent back to the kitchen. In your position you must stand firm.'

'My position, Arthur?' Richard was puzzled.

'Because you, like me, are the son of a country parson, is no reason to put up with the insolence of servants.'

Richard went into the hall wishing his brother was back with his Anthea. He shouted for Mr Hudson. After a while Edward came through the green baize door from the basement.

It appeared Mr Hudson wasn't available, so Edward was told to tell Mrs Bridges about the grit in the sauce.

'Hudson not available,' said Arthur, who had been listening from the door. 'It doesn't surprise me. A furtive looking fellow, with whisky on his breath.'

'Hudson? Furtive?' Richard shook his head and laughed. It was the only thing you could do with Arthur and his theories.

It would have surprised them all if they could have seen the butler at that moment. He was in a small mahogany fitting room trying on a morning suit. As the assistant handed him a grey top hat and a gold handled cane it would not be too much to say that he preened himself in the long mirror.

In the afternoon Violet observed Mr Hudson moving furtively across from the back door to his pantry clutching a large brown paper parcel. She confided the fact to the other junior servants.

'Perhaps he's an anarchist going to blow us all up,' Ruby suggested optimistically.

After Mr Hudson had excused himself for his absence upstairs, Arthur Bellamy produced another theory.

'The man's got a mistress,' he vouchsafed.

'Really, Arthur, your imagination runs away with you,' said Richard.

'You can see it in his eye,' Arthur went on with a professional certainty. 'The sly look of the confirmed lecher.'

'Hudson a lecher?' Richard shrugged. 'The idea is almost laughable.'

Laughable or not a little seed of suspicion had been planted in Richard Bellamy's mind.

'Do you check your cellars? Personally?' Arthur asked. Richard did not, he left it to Hudson. Anthea on the other hand weighed out every day's supplies every morning, high days and holidays. Anthea kept all the cupboards locked always. Anthea and Arthur checked the cellars personally every month.

'Allow me to look after myself,' Richard was at last getting to the end of his temper.

'You put me in my place very nicely,' Arthur complained. 'I'm a no-one; a humble country doctor, not grand enough for the Royal Society. But I hope I retain the commonsense that was both our heritage, but which you seem to have abandoned. The man's a rogue, get rid of him.'

'I will do no such thing,' Richard replied firmly. 'Besides the household is Marjorie's concern,' and by that remark he weakened his cause.

'Hiding behind a woman's skirts. You always did. I remember it well,' Arthur said in a bullying tone. 'Richard's little face peeping out from behind mother.'

Richard Bellamy clenched his teeth. He remembered some things about Arthur. Unspeakable things.

'Tomorrow we check your cellars.'

'We do no such thing,' Richard replied but his voice lacked conviction.

If Richard Bellamy had seen his butler later that evening in full morning dress hailing a cab at the corner of Eaton Square and ordering it to take him to the Savoy Hotel the seed of suspicion might have started to grow apace. The facts of this mystery were not entirely simple. Mr Hudson, too, had a brother, a younger brother called Donald, and they had been brought up together in very poor circumstances in Glasgow and had become very close friends before the need to earn a living had parted their lives at an early age. Angus into service as a houseboy and Donald into the ship building yards on the Clyde. Donald had prospered marvellously. He had worked hard at his talent for engineering and had found rewarding work in the bridge-building line in the Far East. The last time Angus had heard from him was in the form of a wedding invitation, Donald's marriage to a provincial governor's daughter in a cathedral in Malaya. That had been sixteen years before. From these facts it can be deduced that the Hudson brothers were not great letter writers.

The letter from Donald telling his brother that he would be in London and looked forward to the long awaited reunion had come as a considerable shock to the butler. The telegram of the morning had announced the imminent arrival of the Hudson family at the Savoy Hotel.

Poor Mr Hudson was faced with a difficult problem. He was not ashamed of his position as butler to the Bellamy family, in fact, he had often stated aloud and in public that his was a proud and rewarding position in life. Yet the tone of his brother's letter had implied that he thought Angus was rather higher up the ladder of society, considerably higher. This worried Mr Hudson. He didn't want to let Donald down, especially with this new grand wife and daughter.

Mr Hudson had read how much the upkeep of 'face' mattered in the colonies. It wasn't for his own sake that he had decided on the little deception of playing the gentleman but for the sake of his brother Donald.

As he followed a servant down the long corridor of the hotel towards his brother's suite the butler felt a fluttering in the region of his stomach.

He needn't have worried, the welcome he received was almost overwhelmingly enthusiastic. Donald had grown rather portly and florid and lost more of his hair than his brother, a fact which Mr Hudson noted with a feeling akin to complaisance. Maudie, the wife, was a fluttery, gay, friendly sort of woman, overshadowing her rather shy and sullen daughter. Mr Hudson remembered that Miss Elizabeth had been very much the same at that difficult age of fifteen.

'At last I have met my dear, dear brother-in-law, who did so much for my Donald when he was a little boy,' gushed Mrs Donald, holding Mr Hudson's hands with both her own. 'The dear good brother who made my husband what he is, the goodest, kindest, cleverest man in all the world.'

She turned her head sharply like a bird.

'Alice, look out in the corridor,' she commanded. 'Make sure that horrid little page boy didn't leave my other hatbox outside on purpose.'

A sharp turn back to her brother-in-law. 'He had no respect at all. They say the servant problem here is quite terrible—I believe it, I really do.' She opened her big blue eyes as wide as they would go, as if appealing to Mr Hudson to believe that she really did believe it. 'At least in Penang you know who is who by their colour.'

Mrs Donald Hudson was one of those ladies whose mind hopped from one idea to another with such speed that her tongue wasn't always able to keep up with it.

'Well, what are you doing with yourself these days?' Donald asked so suddenly that Angus, who had been dreading the question, was almost taken off his guard.

'I work for Mr Richard Bellamy,' he said. 'The well known Member of Parliament.'

To his surprise they both knew all about the Bellamys. In the colonies the illustrated papers were read from cover to cover. Maudie knew more about Lady Marjorie than Mr Hudson found comfortable; she was an avid reader of the *Sketch* and remembered every fête Lady Marjorie had opened for the last five years, what sort of hat she had worn at Ascot, even the exact date the King had dined at 165 Eaton Place.

'Donald said you were always quite a scholar,' Maudie said admiringly, 'but I had no idea. So distinguished. I would so love an introduction—one is so cut off at home. Donald thinks I'm a snob, but it means so much—a bridge builder after all is only an engineer.'

'Lady Marjorie is away in the country at the moment,'

Angus said quickly, 'and I'm afraid we have the workmen in the house.'

He felt the royal 'we' was forgivable in the circumstances and that he had been quite clever in giving his brother and sister-in-law the impression that he was in a private and confidential position within the charmed circle of a great Tory family, without actually having to tell an untruth.

Such sudden distinction rested lightly on Mr Hudson's morning coated shoulders for he knew the lines and could act the part very well as any good butler can ape his betters. The difficulty was that with such distinction came responsibility. Naturally his sister-in-law took it for granted that he was a rich man with a wide circle of distinguished acquaintances in London. Within a short time he found himself agreeing to take the whole family to 'Our Miss Gibbs' at the Gaiety Theatre and to buy a box into the bargain.

At Maudie Hudson's express request the butler also found himself engaging to book a table for luncheon at Spinelli's, one of the most expensive restaurants in London, for the day after the theatre. He heard with relief that it was to be their last day in England, as that evening they were booked to depart on a steamship for America where Donald was to build yet another bridge.

'Oh Angus, it is all so exciting. You will be able to show us who is who, and perhaps introduce us.' She threw her arms round her husband's neck. 'Who would have thought that my Donald's brother would be so important in the fashionable world?'

Mr Hudson smiled as modestly as he was able.

'It's that black cat. Unlucky,' Mrs Bridges avowed as she

worked at her sewing that evening. 'No one's sent back a sauce of mine since my first place when the cook fell dead over dinner and I had to step right over her and carry on.'

Mrs Bridges sniffed at the memory.

'I was only the kitchen maid then,' she explained. 'They weren't grateful. They sent the hollandaise back, said it was curdled.'

Mrs Bridges tossed her head angrily.

'Well, the look on that poor dead woman's face was enough to curdle anything, it was.'

'As for poor Mr Hudson, I don't know what the matter is,' Miss Roberts chimed in. 'I fear for his sanity. I haven't been spoken to like that since my father saw me walking out with a young man.' Miss Roberts was still smarting from Mr Hudson's remarks about her age and failing abilities made after the discovery of the glove that morning.

'Only ever the one, of course,' she went on, presumably referring to the young man, not the glove. 'They sent me into service and I soon forgot him,' she recalled, 'and I'm very happy, so long as people speak nicely to me. He was a pleasant young man, well set up, but not well spoken, you see.'

Mrs Bridges nodded. For her there was a wealth of meaning in the lady's maid's words.

'It wouldn't have done,' Miss Roberts went on sadly. 'I have always, afterwards, mixed with a very nice class of people. Above stairs, at any rate.'

She knotted the end of the cotton and broke it neatly with her teeth.

'Well one lives as one can, doesn't one.'

Mr Hudson came in from his pantry.

'So you're back, Mr Hudson,' Mrs Bridges remarked rather pointedly.

'I am here, which is what is of significance,' the butler replied at his most dark and metaphysical.

'You seem to be coming and going a great deal lately, Mr Hudson,' said Miss Roberts.

'I have certain personal matters to attend to Miss Roberts,' the implication that he wanted no interference in his private life from the women was clear and unmistakable. To be truthful the nervous strain of the day had taken its toll of Mr Hudson and now financial worries were beginning to cloud his brain.

He nearly dropped the drink tray taking it into the morning room. The incident did not go unnoticed.

'That man is depleted by lust and passion,' Arthur remarked when the butler had withdrawn. 'His eyes are haggard, his face drawn. It is London; how can a man remain pure in this overheated air?'

Arthur was pleased to enlarge on one of his favourite themes.

'Why do you surround yourself with such filth, Richard?' he asked.

Richard Bellamy had been trying to read the *Pall Mall Gazette* and turn his mind away from his brother's conversation.

'Are you still referring to my butler?' he asked in a tired voice.

'Your son sent to the colonies. His doxy harboured under your roof, a scarlet woman.' Arthur began his catalogue of the family troubles with some relish.

'Sarah?' Bellamy was surprised to hear her referred to as

a doxy, let alone a scarlet woman. 'Poor child. The baby died you know.'

'God's mercy on those who least deserved it,' Arthur was quick with the pious retort. 'A daughter separated from her husband after only weeks of marriage. In your circles, such things are a matter of course . . .'

Richard Bellamy prayed silently for patience.

'Hardly,' he replied reasonably. 'And still painful.'

Arthur sniffed. 'And under your roof your servants run riot. Under your roof; the thrashing limbs, the sweat, the foul rankness of animal degradation . . .'

Richard Bellamy had had enough.

'Arthur, for God's sake,' he said testily, and stood up. 'Let's go to bed.'

'You're no judge of character, Richard,' Arthur wasn't going to let go now that he had found a sensitive nerve. 'Never were. Look where it's led you.'

Richard opened the door.

'Are you happy? Are you?' Arthur demanded.

Richard didn't answer.

He didn't sleep well that night and when the butler came in the next morning to ask for the afternoon and the evening off he found that in spite of himself the suspicions so carefully nurtured by his brother were easily aroused.

'You're not in any trouble?' he asked. 'You would feel free to come to me?'

'Oh indeed, sir,' Mr Hudson replied.

'If I say "no",' Bellamy continued.

'It is your right, sir.'

'I had not finished speaking. If I say no, you might simply

take the time off in any case, and I would not know, would I?'

'That is not the way things are, sir,' the butler answered in a hurt voice and Richard Bellamy knew that he was being unjust and petty.

'No.' He turned to his papers. 'Take as much time as you wish. My brother will be here another night. See that his room is comfortable. There seems to be a great deal of dust about.'

'The bells will be connected today,' he explained. 'Then we will be back to normal.'

The butler paused, seeking some way of finding appeasement.

'Would you care for the fire to be lit, sir?' he asked. 'It is a little chilly in here. A fire makes things more cheerful.'

'Leave it as it is,' Bellamy replied without looking up. There was to be no immediate reconciliation.

'I have only thirty pounds,' Mrs Bridges explained, 'a lifetime's savings, but you're welcome to it.'

Mr Hudson was moved and ashamed at having to make his request. Mrs Bridges covered his embarrassment with words.

'I should have more, I know,' she went on. 'But I got carried away by the tales in the Sunday papers, those poor little pagans destined for a lifetime's torment in the burning flames of hell. I gave all of twenty pounds to the Missionary fund.'

As if to make it easier for him to take the money she referred to an incident in the past when he had done her a great service. Mrs Bridges undid the little chamois leather bag and poured out the gold sovereigns; thirty of them. The significance of the number didn't seem to worry either of them. Between the butler and the cook there was no thought of betrayal.

'Only on loan, Kate,' Mr Hudson explained, 'until such time as I can realise my capital.'

'Have it, Angus,' said Mrs Bridges.

'I am only temporarily embarrassed, that's all,' he continued overstating his assurance.

'I don't ask no questions,' Mrs Bridges said frankly, but a thought seemed to strike her at that very moment, an impious thought, 'the horses, was it?' she asked.

'Kate.' The butler was truly shocked at the accusation. 'You know I've never had a wager on a horse.'

'Well,' said Mrs Bridges, and she seemed almost disappointed, 'as long as I see the money again one day, before it's too late. I would like to see a little sun sometime. And winter coming on.' She turned away. 'I don't ask no questions,' she added sadly. 'You've got to trust people, haven't you!'

Mr Hudson knew the parsley sauce was still very much on her mind.

At about the same time as Miss Gertie Miller was taking her sixth curtain call before a delighted audience which included Mr Hudson and all the relations he had in the world, Richard Bellamy and his brother descended the back stairs of 165 Eaton Place, to inspect and indeed inaugurate the new electric bell system. The main installation being in the area of the butler's pantry and the wine cellar, Arthur was able to persuade his brother to inspect and check the wines and spirits at the same time.

To his considerable relief and satisfaction Richard Bellamy

127

found everything in perfect order. He took a bottle of vintage port from its rack to celebrate his butler's vindication.

'A reward for spying on my innocent butler,' he told his brother. But brother Arthur had been playing the detective behind Richard's back. On a pad below the telephone in the butler's pantry he had found the following scribbled words: 'Wed. Gaiety. Box D. Thurs. Spinelli's. 1.15. Table for four.'

'Dammit Arthur, you could persuade an angel the harp he played on was out of tune,' said Richard as they drank the port. 'You nearly persuaded me that my wretched butler was a drunkard, a lecher, a liar and a thief and Lord knows what else.'

'I think I owe you some sort of an apology, Richard,' Arthur replied in what seemed a remarkably contrite tone. 'After putting me up here, to undermine your trust in such a way, I shall make amends.'

'There's no need,' Richard assured him, delighted at the change of heart.

'I shall entertain you to luncheon tomorrow, before I catch my train back to Norfolk,' Arthur suggested, and Richard gladly accepted the invitation.

'We shall go to Spinelli's,' said Arthur with sudden inspiration. 'I haven't been there for years. I'm told one may see all sorts of unexpected people there. It should be interesting, eh?'

Arthur Bellamy was right in his assumption that Spinelli's at lunch time could boast of the most varied and distinguished clientèle in the capital of the British Empire. Maudie Hudson, that keen student of the social magazine, could put a name to almost everyone; there was George Grossmith, the actor they had seen on the boards only the evening before;

Mr Somerset Maugham, the elegant new fashionable drama-tist with four plays running in the West End at the same time; he had the star of 'Lady Frederick' on one side and the star of 'Dot' on the other. There was Sir Edward Carson, the lawyer who had been the solicitor-general in Mr Balfour's Government, lunching in perfect amnesty with his most bitter rival in the advocacy stakes, Mr Marshall Hall. There were a host of others, so many indeed that Maudie Hudson could hardly contain herself, and her brother-in-law sat back with a feeling of complacent satisfaction almost as if all these people had come to present themselves at his bidding.

Mr Hudson's serene, triumphal mood was rudely shat-tered by the sight of Mr Richard and Mr Arthur Bellamy entering the restaurant behind the head waiter. He turned his head aside in fear and shame as his master brushed past him.

'Who is that man who looked at you when he went past, Uncle Angus?' Alice asked with the acute observance and the unerring tactlessness of youth. 'Is he a friend?' When her uncle did not reply immediately she prattled on.

'I have a friend looked like that at me once,' she remarked. 'I'd put honey in her hair. It was so long she could sit on it and of course with the honey . . .'

'What's the matter, Angus?' Maudie was much concerned. 'You've gone as white as a sheet.'

And to add to Mr Hudson's confusion she clapped her hands and shouted 'Boy, boy,' just as if she was back in the Club at Penang.

Richard Bellamy sat with his lips held taut, tightly to-gether as his brother taunted him.

'You see your butler got up as a gentleman, mixing with

people of superior social standing, who for one reason or another he wishes to impress. Can he afford to come here on what you pay him?'

They both knew Mr Hudson could not.

'How pale he became when he saw you,' Arthur continued triumphantly. 'Perhaps he is still capable of remorse? I doubt it. You have allowed him too much licence, for too long. How else can I bring you to see, Richard, the fatal flaw in your character which is no virtue but the worst of vices.'

Richard Bellamy rose to his feet. 'I'm sorry you didn't get elected as a Fellow of the Royal Society, Arthur,' he said to his astonished brother and to his eternal credit walked across to the table where his butler was having luncheon.

'Angus!' he said to Mr Hudson, 'what a pleasant surprise to see you here, won't you introduce me to your friends.'

Afterwards Maudie was to tell gatherings of friends all over the world that their chance meeting with Mr Richard Bellamy was the highlight of the Hudsons' London visit. He was charming, he was tactful, he was flattering and well informed, knowing all about Donald Hudson's considerable bridge building achievements and speaking of them with admiration.

'This has been a malicious and unnecessary act on your part,' Richard said to Arthur when he returned to his own table.

'I think not,' said Arthur with mouth full of soup. 'I am your elder brother. I have a duty towards you. When a man drifts as you drift—it is surely right to rescue him.'

'Right!' Richard Bellamy's voice had the cold snap in it that his political opponents had learned to respect. 'You have no concept of what is right, Arthur, only of what is mean and nasty and self righteous.'

'You can't speak to me like that,' said Arthur indignantly, 'when I am taking you out to luncheon.'

'I will speak to you as I wish.' Richard was not to be baulked. 'You were an abominable bullying self-righteous prig of a small boy and you made my childhood a living hell. If I hid behind mother's skirts it was because you were twice my size . . .' Arthur tried to interrupt but Richard would not allow him.

'I am richer than you, I am happier. I am freer in my mind and in my attitudes than you. I make more effect upon the world, I spread less trouble about me . . .'

He gave a cheerful distant wave to the Hudson party who were leaving.

'This is not to be tolerated,' said Arthur rising. 'Such abuse. Such twisting of hard truth into convenient lies. I do not think we shall see each other again.'

'Neither do I,' his brother agreed succinctly. Arthur put down some money.

'I shall take a cab to Liverpool Street and wait for my train there,' Arthur went on. 'I am obliged to you for putting me up. Pray settle the luncheon bill for me.'

'I will not allow you to pay for a meal to which I was invited for the sole purpose of embarrassing one of my servants,' Richard retorted. 'I am sorry that, as my brother, you were not able to display better manners.'

Arthur had no reply; he took his money and walked out of Richard Bellamy's life for ever.

After the farewells to his family, Hudson returned home ashamed and humiliated. He confessed the whole story to

Mrs Bridges who was shocked, distressed and at the same time fascinated. She had never heard anything like it in her life.

'Of course I will have to resign,' said the butler.

'Yes, I suppose so,' Mrs Bridges admitted; she could see no alternative.

'I can expect no reference.'

Mrs Bridges shrugged. Mr Hudson could certainly expect no reference. He had been caught in the act and no employer could be expected to forgive such a thing.

'Luncheon at Spinelli's,' she mused. 'That's a posh place.' He nodded. 'What was it like?'

'The service was slow; our second waiter had a gravy splash upon his front. There was some trouble with a shortage of Yorkshire pudding.'

In spite of the stress the professional eye had remained observant.

'One waiter ran, Mrs Bridges.'

'Ran, I never did, Mr Hudson.'

'I believe he was foreign.'

It explained a lot.

'And the food?' Mrs Bridges was deliberately fishing.

'You do better, Kate.'

It was what she wanted to hear but it somehow made the imminent loss of her old friend more unbearable.

'I know,' she replied quietly. 'Oh, Angus, what a dreadful thing you have done. If Lady Marjorie gets to hear of it and hear she will . . . she's expected back this evening.'

This was news to Mr Hudson.

'Yes, there was a message. Mrs Kirbridge is ready to go into the nursing home to have her baby.'

Mr Hudson shook his head. He didn't approve of children

being born in nursing homes, yet he was glad that Lady Marjorie was coming back so soon. His despatch would be swift and clean in her hands—like the guillotine.

'Oh Kate,' said the butler, 'it seems like the end of my life. I feel like a felon under sentence of death. Mr Bellamy has shown me nothing but kindness and consideration and how have I paid him?' He nodded his head. 'I should have spoken the truth while there was still time.'

'You didn't exactly tell a lie, did you?' said the cook trying to find some fact in mitigation.

'I lived one for a wee while,' the butler confessed, 'and the worst of it was, I enjoyed it.'

'And now you'll be punished.'

'Yes.'

'That's life. You get paid out for every bit of happiness.' It was one of Mrs Bridges' favourite aphorisms. 'I sometimes wonder what awful sin we committed in the beginning.'

'Ah well,' said Mr Hudson, 'perhaps my downfall will serve as an example to the others, not to forget their places.'

The morning room bell rang and Mr Hudson put his tail coat on and prepared to meet his fate.

'Whatever you've done, you're a good man, Angus,' Mrs Bridges whispered hoarsely, overcome by the emotion of the moment, 'and that's a fact.' She touched his hand as he passed by.

Her words and her touch remained with Mr Hudson during the long, long walk, from the pantry up the stairs to the morning room.

Mr Bellamy was reading some Parliamentary papers leaning against the fireplace.

'You rang, sir,' said Mr Hudson, in a graveyard voice.

133

Mr. Bellamy seemed not to hear. There was an ominous silence.

'Her ladyship will be arriving shortly,' he observed at last.

'So I understand, sir.'

Mr Bellamy put down the papers and turned to the butler with something like a sigh.

'So you are the brother of Donald Hudson, the great engineer,' he said. 'You kept that very quiet.'

'Sir . . .' the butler began.

'You keep many things quiet, I think.'

'Yes, sir.'

'In point of fact, Hudson, I was very pleased to meet your brother. . . .'

Having decided on his own fate, Mr Hudson was not to be sidetracked.

'I am a servant,' he went on in a low voice, 'but I am also a man. I am humiliated enough, sir. I am wounded. You twist the knife in the wound. There is no need.'

Mr Bellamy raised his hands and opened his palms; he was quite taken aback.

'I will pack my things and leave at once, sir. I do not think you will wish me to work out my notice.' Now that he was launched, Mr Hudson wanted to put an end to the whole thing quickly.

Bellamy shook his head in a confused manner.

'What are you talking about?' he demanded. 'What is the matter with you?'

'In front of your family,' Mr Hudson went on, savouring the very dregs of remorse, 'I must ask you . . . I cannot even request a reference.'

Richard Bellamy looked at the abject creature in front of

him. This Hudson would never span the mighty Zambezi or marry the Governor's daughter.

'Families are very trying,' he confided to the butler. 'I agree. They make us more emotional than they should. My own brother's visit has left me somewhat at a loss. But Hudson, if you wish to visit the theatre or lunch at a fashionable restaurant your money's as good as the next man's, your appearance better than most.'

'This is altogether too liberal a view, sir,' Mr Hudson replied, unwilling to be forgiven without a fight. 'A servant is a servant and must know his place, or the world would crumble about our ears . . .'

Bellamy smiled; when people referred to 'the world' how often they meant their own very small one.

'A man must have his own view of himself,' Mr Bellamy admitted, 'be he master or servant, right or wrong. There is a dignity in that; you are quite right. I assume you had your reasons for acting as you did?'

'It was for the sake of others,' Mr Hudson was pleased to confess. He coughed. 'You . . . you checked the cellars, I believe, sir.'

'I did. They were quite in order,' said Bellamy taking out his handkerchief.

'Of course, sir.'

'Of course indeed,' Bellamy replied. 'Let us say my trust in my fellow men flagged for a while. It has returned.'

Mr Hudson appreciated this frank apology. He began to feel much more himself again.

'By and large, sir, I enjoyed my brother's visit,' he admitted retreating towards the door. 'I am very proud of him.'

Mr Bellamy nodded thoughtfully.

'And I enjoyed my brother's departure,' he replied. 'Alas, he is not proud of me.'

The front door bell rang in the distance and Edward's steps could be heard in the hall.

'Perhaps you had better go and open the door for your mistress,' Mr Bellamy suggested.

The sight of Lady Marjorie and her daughter being greeted by Mr Bellamy, Rose's happy smile of welcome, the familiar luggage brought in by Thomas and Edward, the Rolls Royce in its usual place outside the front door; these things restored Mr Hudson's world, so lately lying shattered in ruins, to its usual comfortable and orderly place in the universe.

CHAPTER NINE

'Mrs Kirbridge is the mother of a little baby girl,' Mr Hudson announced. 'A little baby girl.'

'Is the mother all right?' Sarah asked anxiously. She had only just returned from her nurse's instruction course and was very keen to sound professional.

'I presume so,' the butler replied.

'Isn't that just like a man,' said Mrs Bridges scornfully. 'Didn't even ask what weight it was, I suppose.' Mr Hudson had to admit an omission in this area.

'Bring four bottles of ale, Edward,' he commanded. 'Mr Bellamy asked us to wet the baby's head. After all,' he added smiling, 'it is a bit of an occasion.'

'I bet it was more than "a bit of an occasion" when you was delivered Mr Hudson,' said Sarah. 'We're only born once, you know,' Mrs Bridges added as a corollary.

'I don't recall much of it myself, Mrs Bridges. I was very young at the time.'

If Mr Hudson's humour was a trifle ponderous it was nevertheless welcome for its rarity.

'Ooh Mr Hudson, you *are* a wag,' roared Mrs Bridges, and Edward brought in the ale.

When it came to the toast Mr Hudson didn't even know the baby's name. It later transpired that the latest addition to the Bellamy family was to be christened Lucy and while she was being toasted upstairs and downstairs, Sarah went

137

up and put on her nursemaid's uniform to further celebrate the occasion.

She looked extremely smart in her pale grey uniform, starched apron and small white starched cap.

'Blimey,' said Edward when he saw her.

'Blimey is right,' Mrs Bridges agreed, her speech a little affected by the strong ale. 'What's all this in aid of, my girl?'

'It's my official nurse's uniform. That's what it's in aid of,' Sarah answered proudly. 'My official nursemaid's uniform.'

In spite of the fact that Mrs Kirbridge and the baby would be in the nursing home for at least another week nothing could persuade Sarah to take off her uniform.

'My official duties start from the day the baby is born,' she explained adamantly. 'I've got to get the nursery floor all ready for the homecoming.'

This in spite of the fact that the nursery floor had just been decorated from top to toe and was as ready as any nursery floor in London.

'I'm glad it's a girl, because of the clothes,' Sarah explained. 'You really can dress a girl.'

'Most women want boys, my girl,' said Mrs Bridges, with worldly wisdom. 'Most women wouldn't say thank you for a girl, I can tell you. Not first off.'

'In the circumstances, it's probably just as well,' Miss Roberts remarked sourly. It was also just as well that only Thomas and Rose even suspected who was the real father of the child.

'It's a pity there's not more babies born in this household,' said Mrs Bridges, pouring out some more ale. 'I could do with some of this every day. Keep me going.'

'I wouldn't mind if there was one born every minute,' said

Sarah dreamily. 'I'd look after them all, I would really. I'd be the best nursery nurse in the whole wide world.'

She shook her head. 'I'm not half going to look after that little baby,' she promised them.

'I'm sure you'll be an excellent nurserymaid,' Miss Roberts said in her cold voice.

'Miss Elizabeth will really be proud,' said Sarah.

'And doubtless you'll be a great help to Nanny,' Miss Roberts went on.

'There isn't going to be no Nanny,' Sarah replied sharply, furious at Miss Roberts' mocking, taunting tone.

'No?' said Miss Roberts, meaning 'Yes.'

'What do you think I've been trained for then?' Sarah demanded angrily. 'What was all the training for then, if it wasn't for looking after the baby?'

'For helping,' Miss Roberts explained patiently. 'Nurse-maids are there to help the Nanny.'

The seeds of doubt had been planted in Sarah's mind. 'There was no mention made,' she said without conviction.

'Well, you obviously know best,' said Miss Roberts. She turned to Mrs Bridges very deliberately. 'As if a family like this would do without a Nanny,' she said.

Nanny Webster arrived two days later. 'You can almost hear the house shaking already,' Richard Bellamy said to his wife. He still had vivid memories of Nanny from his own children's nursery days.

Nanny had nursed Lady Marjorie in her youth, as well as her brother Lord Ashby and her children, James and Elizabeth. She had retired in her old age to a cottage in Southwold village. There Lady Marjorie had paid her a visit earlier in the summer as she always did when she went to

Southwold. She hadn't asked Nanny to come up to London to look after Elizabeth's baby, Nanny Webster had taken it for granted and Lady Marjorie hadn't the heart to forbid it. After all even though the old lady was well over seventy she was ageless in the manner of her kind; a big, rawboned, strong woman with a gaunt face, made more severe by the black Victorian clothes she always wore.

When Mr Hudson opened the door and saw the familiar figure standing on the step and looked again into the piercing critical eyes his heart sank.

'I had to ring twice,' were Nanny's first words to the butler. 'I hope that is not a symptom of domestic disorder.'

Mr Hudson was quick to deny any such thing.

'I see you've taken to wearing glasses, Hudson,' Nanny went on, inspecting him closely. 'Of course you must be getting quite old now.'

Nanny walked into the hall and looked round.

'These small town houses,' she muttered and turned again to the butler. 'I hope everything is in order, Hudson,' she warned him. 'For instance the area is hardly the place for the baby's perambulator. It will rust in the wet weather. See it is kept in the front hall in future.'

Thus the battle was joined at an early stage between the nursery and the kitchen floors. The instruction concerning the perambulator was particularly hurtful to Mr Hudson because only two days before having barked his shins on the wretched thing cluttering up the front hall, he himself had ordered Edward to banish it to the area.

Nanny didn't approve of the choice of Sarah to be her nurserymaid, but knowing the reason for Sarah's presence in the house at Eaton Place she was forced to accept Lady Marjorie's decision and to have the girl on trial.

Nanny didn't approve of the nurseries either. She disliked the modern light paint and the animal frieze above the rail, speaking scathingly of fashionable interior decorators; she frowned at the gas fire—'Burns up all the good in the air.' She threw her hands up at the geyser—'A monstrous device. Highly dangerous.' The linoleum she found uncomfortable, cold and slippery and she exploded at the sight of feeding bottles, holding it as a basic rule of midwifery that the mother should breast feed her baby. It was a relief to Sarah when Nanny turned her attention to the kitchen.

It is a basic fact of life that nannies dislike cooks and cooks hate nannies but with Nanny Webster and Mrs Bridges it was something deeper; a long, almost forgotten, duel was now to be renewed. When Sarah came down with a message from Nanny that in future all fat was to be cut from her meat Mrs Bridges' loins were already girded metaphorically speaking and she was ready.

'Who does she think she blooming well is?' Mrs Bridges demanded loudly of the servants' hall. 'The Duchess of Southwold or something? If *she* imagines I've got nothing better to do than to sit around cutting the fat off her meat, she must be mad.' She turned to Mr Hudson with a knowing look. 'She hasn't changed,' she said.

The arrival of the baby didn't alter things very much for the better as Sarah had been hoping. True there was little Lucy herself to keep them all busy but Nanny was extraordinary with the baby, both clumsy and jealous of Sarah touching her. For the first few days Sarah was content just to sit and watch in wonder that such a tiny little thing could actually exist on this earth.

After the christening outside the church Elizabeth handed the baby to Sarah to hold as Nanny was nowhere to be seen. When she did come up Sarah was whispering sweet nothings as she gently rocked the child.

'Don't you be so familiar with Baby,' Nanny told her testily seizing Lucy quite roughly. 'It is Baby to you, not little Lucy or anything else. It is not your place to be familiar with Baby. You're to have no part of her, you understand? No part at all.'

Nanny's temper was not improved by her losing the battle of the breast feeding. Elizabeth would not feed it and that was that. One morning Sarah had prepared the warm milk and put the bottle ready for Nanny when the old woman knocked it off the table and Sarah caught it as it fell.

'You clumsy girl!' Nanny shouted at her. 'Can't you do anything right? You're very lucky it didn't break.'

Sarah was stung into answering back this flagrant piece of injustice. 'But Nanny it was you,' she replied unwisely.

Nanny Webster turned on her furiously. 'Now listen to me, girl,' she hissed, 'one more instance of your impertinence, one more instance of your appalling, slovenly ways, and I shall have you dismissed.'

Sarah had been taught on her course of instruction that the first duty of a nurserymaid was to be loyal to Nanny but in the circumstances it became more and more difficult.

There was no one to turn to for help. Elizabeth had become ill after the christening and was in bed with an anaemic condition and was not to be disturbed under any condition. Lady Marjorie was staying down at Southwold as her father had suffered a heart attack and was gravely ill and Thomas Watkins was with her. As for the other servants, they got on Sarah's nerves. One day Mrs Bridges was having one of her tantrums over a complaint Nanny had sent down about the sweet at lunch time.

It took all Mr Hudson's persuasive powers to prevent the cook taking up her rolling pin and confronting Nanny with it then and there.

'Let her stew in her own juice,' Edward suggested helpfully.

'That's the general idea, Edward,' Mr Hudson agreed, although they were not the words he would have chosen himself.

'Perhaps you're right,' Mrs Bridges said, calming down a little. 'But I'm having no more complaints.' She wagged her finger at Sarah. It annoyed Sarah strangely.

'You lot,' she said, looking at them in utter contempt and folding her arms. 'Really! All you lot is concerned about is whether Nanny leaves the fat off of her meat and doesn't like stupid blackberry and apple pie.'

'Such eloquence!' said Rose who was passing the door but had come in hearing the sounds of discord.

'Not whether she's a fit person and proper person to look after little children,' Sarah continued. In her state of anxiety for the baby it didn't occur to Sarah that the Nanny's suitability was no real concern of the other servants.

'We thought that was your concern,' said Rose. 'Your private territory.'

'For all you lot care she could be dropping the baby on its head and feeding it neat gin. For all you lot care!'

Seeing the argument was developing into a silly female

quarrel, Mr Hudson stepped in. He told them he would have no more of it.

'We have a house to run,' he told them, 'and we must make sure that it is run efficiently.'

'And I suppose that means a little baby has to learn to run efficiently,' said Sarah bitterly. Mr Hudson frowned. 'So that she can fit into your nice pattern of things. Into the well run household.'

'Sarah,' said Mr Hudson firmly, 'I have had quite enough of your melodramatics. You dramatise everything quite out of proportion, and since you are constantly reminding us that you are no longer in the employ of the kitchen floor I would be extremely grateful if you would confine the dramas of the nursery floor to where they belong. The nursery.'

Sarah had cried wolf once too often. Mr Hudson remembering the many times he had succumbed to Sarah's play acting in the past would have no more of it.

Early the next morning Sarah was awakened by the sound of Lucy's crying; to her ears there was something unusual in the sound, something desperate. Sarah put on her dressing gown and tiptoed into the night nursery. Nanny was lying on her back snoring and the baby was lying half under her, nearly suffocated. Sarah managed to lift the child and took it across and put it in its own cot. At breakfast time Nanny made no comment. She clearly didn't even miss the child beside her when she awoke.

All the morning Sarah kept trying to screw herself up to go in to see Elizabeth Kirbridge. A chance remark by Rose that Miss Elizabeth was better and had sent for her dressmaker, made her mind up for her.

Elizabeth was in bed reading when Sarah came in.

'Well, Sarah,' she said. 'What do you want?'

'It's about Nanny, madam,' Sarah began. 'Well about me and Nanny—and the baby. I don't want to bother you,' Sarah went on, 'but it's a bit urgent.'

'Well what is it?' said Elizabeth with a sigh.

'Nanny,' Sarah explained. 'It's not just that she's old, there's nothing wrong in being old. It's that she doesn't seem to be able to manage proper.' She paused and then added, 'the way you would wish, madam. She's just not suitable for a baby. Not for a little baby, really she isn't.'

'And are you suitable?' Elizabeth replied impatiently. 'Really, Sarah, who could be more suitable than Nanny. You are talking nonsense. I want no more tales from the nursery floor.'

'I just wish you would have a word with her,' said Sarah.

'Sarah,' Elizabeth said severely, 'the very reason for Nanny Webster being here is so that I do not have to keep going to "have a word with her". I am not well, do you understand?'

'I'm sorry, madam,' said Sarah, 'but it's your baby and you've hardly seen her since you've been home.'

Elizabeth's eyes flashed in anger.

'You impudent, impertinent girl,' she began . . .

Sarah interrupted.

'I'm sorry,' she said quietly, 'it's just—it's just that I love that baby like it was my very own.'

Elizabeth drew in her breath. Sarah could have found no better way to remind Elizabeth of her own lack of love for the child. The greater part of her illness was caused by her own mental condition aggravated by the shock of the child-birth. Lucy alive and well and growing in the same house

seemed to her to be a perpetual reminder of her own behaviour on the night the child was conceived.

'You mean you'd like to make her your own?' she said
in a hard voice.

'No,' Sarah protested. It didn't seem any good arguing
anymore.

'I'm sorry, Sarah,' Elizabeth went on. 'I'm tired still. I'm
tired of people coming in and out of my room all day long
with various stupid theories about babies and what to do
with them and what not to do with them.'

Sarah found this strange because as far as she knew this
was the first time anyone had talked to Elizabeth Kirbridge
about her baby.

'I'm just very tired,' Elizabeth complained. 'Perhaps you
don't fully realise just how tired one feels after you've had
a baby.'

Even as she said it she realised this was a cruel thought-
less remark she had just made.

'Yes,' Sarah said bluntly. 'I know how you feel, Miss
Elizabeth, and it's because I know how you feel I don't want
nothing to happen to that baby.'

'I'm sorry Sarah,' Elizabeth said contritely. 'I was thought-
less. I should have remembered.'

'There's nothing left to remember now,' Sarah replied in
a quiet voice.

Elizabeth stopped thinking about herself and her heart
went out to Sarah. She closed her book.

'Sarah,' she said. 'Sit down.' She patted the side of her
bed and Sarah sat down on it. 'Tell me.'

Sarah told her everything.

146

Elizabeth had never been one of Nanny Webster's favourite charges and as she went into her own nursery she felt a familiar, long forgotten chill down her spine.

Nanny was muttering to the baby and didn't see or hear Elizabeth at first.

'Nanny,' said Elizabeth.

Nanny jumped round, startled. 'We like people to knock on the door before they come in,' she said reprovingly. 'People creeping up behind a person can make something silly occur.'

'Sorry, Nanny,' said Elizabeth.

'Nursery discipline is nursery discipline, Miss Elizabeth,' Nanny went on as she put the baby in her cot, 'and everyone must observe it.'

'Of course, Nanny, I understand,' said Elizabeth sitting down.

'I should be surprised if you do,' Nanny grumbled. 'Remembering your ideas of tidiness, I should be surprised if you have any notion at all of what I'm talking about.'

She gave Elizabeth that well remembered look of disapproval and Elizabeth took her elbows off the table with automatic guilt.

'I understand, Nanny,' she said.

'You've never been one for babies, Miss Elizabeth,' Nanny went on. 'You couldn't possibly understand. Other little girls loved their dolls but not Elizabeth. You'd always rather be playing with the dogs or scrambling up trees, tearing your clothes and making yourself filthy.'

Whenever Elizabeth tried to bring the conversation round to the subject of little Lucy and Nanny's ability to look after her, Nanny Webster turned it to Elizabeth's own shortcomings and her disappointing married life. After a while Elizabeth gave up the unequal task and went downstairs to telephone to her mother.

Although old Lord Southwold was still gravely ill, Lady Marjorie came back to London immediately. She knew that she was the only person who could cope with old Nanny and deal with a situation which was greatly of her own making. In fact she had been fearing exactly what had happened would happen ever since Nanny Webster's arrival.

'I've a host of things to do in the nursery,' Nanny said warily to Lady Marjorie when they were sat in the morning room having coffee. 'I've little time to sit around gossiping.'

Nanny was no fool and she knew well enough what Lady Marjorie's sudden return portended.

While Lady Marjorie talked of the difficulties and complications of a nursery in London, Nanny would have none of it and grumbled about incompetent gossiping nursemaids.

As Lady Marjorie watched Nanny feeling about for her coffee spoon her heart went out to the old woman, fighting a losing battle against her blindness and yet far too obstinate to give way to wearing glasses.

'Nanny dear,' said Lady Marjorie, 'you see I was afraid of this; of it proving too much for you. It was grossly unfair of me to drag you out of retirement without explaining properly that I only wanted you to supervise as it were.'

'Supervise indeed?' Nanny snorted. 'I have been a nanny all my life, not a supervisor whatever that may be.' Nanny's mind seemed to wander. 'I nannied you when you were only a little girl . . . you were always beautiful. Always my favourite child.'

Lady Marjorie stretched out and touched Nanny's wrinkled old hand in a gesture of affection.

'I know you would soldier on, under all these difficulties without ever saying a word, but I blame myself for not considering all the problems. Particularly the stairs,' said Lady Marjorie.

The stairs were a happy inspiration on Lady Marjorie's part for they gave Nanny a valid yet honourable excuse to retire without either her eyesight or her ability to cope in the nursery being brought into question.

'You've been listening to tittle tattle, child. Your mother always ignored servants' gossip on principle,' she said, but the fire had gone out of her complaint.

Lady Marjorie seized the opportunity to enlarge further on the steepness of the stairs in London houses.

'The stairs I'm afraid, are a bit much for me,' Nanny admitted at last. 'Of course nurserymaids are the worst source of gossip I know.' It was the last shot in her locker.

The day Nanny departed Elizabeth went up to the nursery and watched Sarah giving Lucy her tea. Mrs Bridges passed the day without a single cross word to Ruby and Mr Hudson gave orders for the perambulator to be banished once more from the front hall. It was as if a cloud had been lifted from 165 Eaton Place.

After many interviews and checking of references, Lady Marjorie and Elizabeth engaged Nanny Wright. She was comfortable and middle-aged and quite happy to supervise while the nurserymaid did the hard work and the chores. She never complained of Mrs Bridges' cooking as long as there was plenty of it and she thoroughly approved of the modern labour saving arrangements in the nurseries. She was exactly what was wanted at 165 Eaton Place.

For her good services Sarah was rewarded with an increase in her wages from eighteen to twenty pounds a year.

CHAPTER TEN

Lord Southwold died in the fullness of his years and was buried among his ancestors. Old Lady Southwold and Miss Hodges, her companion, came to stay in London for the Memorial Service in Westminster Abbey. The King was represented by the Prince and Princess of Wales and the servants' hall of 165 Eaton Place by Mr Hudson, Mrs Bridges and Rose, all of whom had started their life in service at Southwold House. Nanny Wright and little Lucy were away at the seaside and Sarah was left to look after the nurseries. Before dinner she took the perambulator across to the garage for Thomas to mend a broken spoke only to find the chauffeur had a smart visitor, a Mr Donaldson, who talked about nothing but motor cars.

It wasn't until she had her afternoon rest that Lady Southwold discovered that her diamond and ruby butterfly brooch was missing. It had been given to her by Lord Southwold on her birthday the year before and was therefore especially precious. Lady Marjorie and Miss Hodges searched the bedroom but they could find no trace of it.

'It has been taken,' said Lady Southwold leaving no room at all for argument.

When Richard Bellamy came back from Westminster his wife and Miss Hodges sought his guidance in the matter.

'I take it the police are going to be informed,' said Miss Hodges.

'No need for that yet,' Richard Bellamy told her. 'We can usually sort out our own difficulties and I'm sure Lady Southwold wouldn't wish it.'

Nothing could have a more disturbing and demoralising effect on a household than to have the police asking questions and putting everyone under suspicion.

Miss Hodges was one of those sad, ill-favoured young women for whom life is a constant burden. She had no money and little charm and yet had pretensions to being a lady with none of the attributes. She was consistently rude and off-hand with servants for fear she might be taken for one herself.

'I didn't like to speak when Lady Marjorie was present,' she said to Richard Bellamy when his wife had gone up to change for dinner, 'but I think I may be able to shed some light on this unfortunate affair.'

She went on to explain that she had found Miss Roberts in what now seemed suspicious circumstances on her return from the Abbey that morning. 'The door of Lady Southwold's room was open. Roberts could have been coming out,' she explained. 'She appeared shifty and offered no adequate explanation when I asked her what her business was.'

Richard Bellamy helped himself to a whisky and soda and sat down to think. After a while he rang for Mr Hudson. If anyone could sort out the problem without too much fuss it was the butler.

'Just a few discreet enquiries, Hudson, not a full-scale investigation,' Mr Bellamy advised. 'I don't want alarm and despondency. Do you think you can handle it?'

'I'll do my best,' Mr Hudson replied in a subdued manner.

Mr Hudson went to his pantry and lit a pipe, a thing he

hadn't done for years. Doubtless it was in unconscious imitation of the great Mr Holmes. After a few minutes he wrote out a list.

'Suspects. Edward, Ruby, Violet, Sarah. Miss Roberts (Miss Hodges' statement).'

Already the news of the missing brooch was creating excitement and whisperings among the servants.

'We are all under suspicion,' Miss Roberts told the servants' hall at supper.

'Not all of us, Miss Roberts,' Mrs Bridges reminded her smugly. 'Not those as went to the Abbey.'

After supper Mr Hudson started his enquiry, questioning each of the servants on his list in turn. When it came to Sarah she couldn't be found and Rose was despatched to fetch her. She found her in the garage talking to Thomas, her excuse being that she was fetching the pram.

'What's it about?' Sarah asked.

'What do you think it's about?' Rose answered coldly. 'Go on, hurry up, he's waiting.'

When Sarah had gone Rose stayed behind. It was high time she had it out with Mr Thomas Watkins and she just felt in the mood.

'What do you want, Rosie?' Thomas asked in a friendly way. 'Something on your mind?'

'Sarah,' Rose answered in a flat voice.

Thomas raised his eyebrows pretending to be puzzled.

'She's spending too much time over here. Mr Hudson doesn't approve,' said Rose, but Thomas knew it was Rose that didn't approve. 'She might get into trouble, that's all. I'm sure you wouldn't want that.'

'No. Well neither of us would want that, would we?'

Thomas replied gravely. 'Caring about her as we do . . .' He turned and began to climb the narrow stairs up to his bedroom.

'What do you mean by that?' Rose demanded. He didn't reply so she followed him up.

'What do you mean by that?' she asked again.

'What I say, Rose.'

He deliberately stripped off his shirt and started to wash his body as if to taunt her.

'I don't know what to make of you, Thomas,' she said half frightened. 'I don't understand you. You were always —twisty.'

'Twisty,' said Thomas thoughtfully.

'Before you came here. At Greenwich. You always got what you wanted.'

Thomas looked at her quizzically. 'I didn't get you,' he said.

'Well . . .' Rose replied turning away, 'that was because you didn't want me.'

'Didn't I?' Thomas sounded surprised.

'All I'm saying is,' Rose went on, trying to get the conversation away from dangerous topics, 'don't ruin Sarah's life; she's done silly things in the past and she's paid for them, and now she's got things straight she doesn't want you to go leading her astray. Do you understand?'

Thomas was washing his neck in the basin.

'She's like a sister to me and I don't want to see her getting hurt by someone like you.'

'That's a proper sisterly concern you're showing too, Rose,' Thomas said in a cold voice as he turned to her. 'By "leading her astray" I take it you mean going to bed with her, do you?'

It wasn't what Rose had meant at all but he knew it would hurt her.

'That as well as other things,' she said.

Thomas seized her roughly by the arm. 'What other things?'

'There's a brooch missing in case you hadn't heard,' she spat at him frightened and sarcastic, 'and she's the obvious one, isn't she?'

'Well she would be pleased to hear that coming from you, Rose,' Thomas replied. 'Her sisterly best friend. You think she stole it for me, is that it?' He shook her hard. 'You think I made her, is that it?' He threw Rose away from him and she stumbled onto her knees.

'You got a nasty mind, Rose,' he sneered. 'A nasty dirty enquiring mind and you can take it out of here fast before I lose my temper.'

She scrambled to her feet and turned at bay. He flicked the end of the towel and hit her with it on the face.

'Get out of my room, will you?' The cold fury in Thomas' voice really frightened Rose.

By the time Mr Hudson was ready to see Miss Roberts, the lady's maid, having heard rumors of Miss Hodges' accusations, had worked herself up into a 'regular state' as Mrs Bridges described it.

'What's that vicious woman been saying about me?' she demanded bursting into the pantry and slamming the door. 'What lies has she been spreading?'

Mr Hudson was quite taken aback and for a moment he was speechless.

'I hadn't been in Lady Southwold's room,' Miss Roberts

went on just as if the butler had already accused her of the theft. 'I'd only looked in to see if anyone was there.'

She was feeling in her sleeve for her handkerchief which Mr Hudson rightly interpreted as a sign of danger.

'Miss Roberts . . .' he began, but was immediately shouted down.

'It's her. She's done it and she's trying to blame me. Has anyone questioned her?'

Miss Roberts raised an accusing finger.

'Please calm yourself, Miss Roberts,' Mr Hudson begged, but Miss Roberts was not the least inclined to be calm. Quite the opposite. She was just coming to the boil. Now she poured out a long tirade castigating Miss Hodges and all her kind for their manifold sins and wickednesses.

'It's only the money they're after,' she said, sitting down suddenly and beginning to sob.

'Miss Hodges has been with Lady Southwold for over ten years,' Mr Hudson replied reasonably enough.

'Ten years,' shrieked Miss Roberts, causing quite a flutter among the other servants listening at the closed door. 'And how long have I been here? Seventeen years! Is that to count for nothing? Is my whole life to be tossed aside on the word of a scheming stranger?'

Mr Hudson put out his hand to calm her but Miss Roberts threw it aside and rushed out of the room crying loudly to the great diversion of the other servants.

For a moment Mr Hudson appeared in the servants' hall door looking hot and flustered.

'You been questioning Miss Roberts then, Mr Hudson?' said Mrs Bridges, and the implication that Miss Roberts had been little less than tortured was clear in her voice.

Mr Hudson shut the door of his pantry and sighed. He was reminded of Mr Gilbert's immortal words, 'A policeman's lot is not a happy one.'

Sarah rushed across to the garage to tell Thomas the latest news of the mystery. He wasn't in the workshop where she'd expected to find him. He was in his bedroom lying on his bed in trousers and vest reading a motoring paper and dreaming of the garage that he was going to run with Mr Donaldson's help.

'Sorry,' said Sarah rather surprised and breathless. 'I didn't know you had gone to bed.'

'I haven't gone to bed,' Thomas explained.

'Just came to tell you they got the thief,' she went on. 'It's Miss Roberts. She confessed to Mr Hudson. You never heard such goings on . . . funny it should be her. I didn't like her very much but I feel sorry for her.'

Thomas opened his mouth and wetted his lips with his tongue. Sarah was just the sort of girl to make a man happy in his lonely bed.

'What a life, eh?' Sarah continued, 'all them years of devoted sewing and hairdressing and packing cases and nowhere to go. Just a lonely old spinster. Poor cow, they say it can make you peculiar going without . . .'

Although she had been aware of Thomas coming up behind her, Sarah didn't move. He seized her, turned her round and kissed her fiercely.

'Is that what they say, now?' he said.

'No!' Sarah drew away.

'What's the matter?' Thomas was surprised and hurt. 'It's what you came for, isn't it? I mean it's provocation coming to a man's bedroom at night time.'

'It isn't late,' Sarah replied. 'It's only nine o'clock.'

'Early to bed, early to rise, eh?' Thomas emphasised his meaning by pressing gently against Sarah.

'What will Rose say?' Sarah asked. 'She'll miss me; she'll wonder where I am.'

Not for the first time Thomas wondered what was the exact nature of the hold Rose seemed to have over Sarah. He had heard that a lot of strange things went on in the crowded attics of Mayfair and Belgravia. It was a common subject of conversation among the footmen in the pub round the corner. Rose wasn't going to get in his way this time.

'You don't have to stay the night here,' he said and kissed her again.

'That's true,' said Sarah and immediately began to tear off her clothes.

'Here wait a minute,' Thomas said, taking her arms and stopping her. 'What's the hurry?'

Instead he began to unbutton and unhook her himself and as each new part of Sarah's shapely body was revealed it occurred to Thomas that there could be fewer more delectable objects in the world than a warm and amorous nurserymaid.

After upstairs dinner was over and cleared away, Mr Hudson decided to take Mrs Bridges and Rose into his confidence and widen the scope of his enquiries by asking them their opinion of the theft.

Mrs Bridges was strong for Sarah being the guilty party although there was no evidence to support her theory.

'You never know with Sarah,' she said, 'and she's been a bit restless lately.'

'What do you think, Rose?' Mr Hudson asked the housemaid. 'You know her best.'

Rose was still smarting from the end of Thomas' towel.

'Sarah wouldn't do it, not on her own,' she replied with conviction. 'But she might be talked into it—by another influence.'

She lowered her voice and looked round carefully, causing the others to lean towards her.

'I mean, she's been keeping a lot of company with Mr Thomas Watkins lately,' Rose whispered.

Mrs Bridges bridled. She wasn't having Rose or anyone else speak slightingly of her Thomas.

'Whatever gave you that idea?' she asked crossly.

'It's not just an idea, Mrs B. There's evidence,' Rose went on. 'There's been a visitor round to see Thomas. A man.'

Mr Hudson frowned thoughtfully. 'You think Sarah might have taken the brooch, given it to Thomas,' he began . . .

'. . . who in turn gets rid of it to a criminal of the under-world,' Rose continued.

'A fence she means,' Mrs Bridges explained. The greater part of her reading was detective fiction and there was little she didn't know about the ways of the underworld.

Rose watched Mr Hudson carefully. She saw doubt creep across his face. He took out his watch and looked at it, a characteristic gesture when he was thinking.

'Fetch Mr Watkins please, Rose,' he said with abrupt formality. 'I wish to talk to him.'

Rose went across to the garage with fear in her heart yet the desire to get the better of Thomas drove her on. When she got to the stairs she could hear voices from the bedroom. She tiptoed half way up.

'My eldest brother, Gwyn. He had the cycle shop I worked in.' It was Thomas' voice. ' "I'll come back and buy you up

159

so you can sit on your backside," that was his parting shot. So it's pride you see.'

For a moment Rose thought it must be a male visitor up there with Thomas. The sound of Sarah's high laugh told her she was wrong.

'That's what I felt with this house,' said Sarah. 'I left once —through the front door, thinkin' I'd show them. But I didn't. They picked me up like a lost blinkin' pet and brought me back.'

Rose clenched her teeth. Although it was Sarah's voice all right, she had to look.

She crept up to the door. There was quite a little hole where an eye in the wood had fallen out. Sarah's long hair was half covering Thomas' naked body.

Rose told Mr Hudson that Thomas had gone to bed and then went up to her room and wept. Tears of jealousy; tears of frustration; tears of hate and self-pity, and tears of shame.

After breakfast the next day Mr Hudson had a most unsatisfactory interview with Thomas Watkins. The chauffeur firmly refused to divulge to the butler the name of his male visitor.

'I don't see I have to tell you who it is,' he said. 'It's a free country. I can entertain who I please.'

Mr Hudson found the words tantamount to mutiny. He pressed Thomas further but again received a blunt negative.

'Then I must draw my own conclusions,' he said huffily.

'You can draw whatever damn conclusions you like,' Thomas replied at the door. He wasn't going to be bullied by the butler. 'It's of no interest to me.'

Mr Hudson hurried upstairs to tell his master the latest developments and Richard Bellamy sent for the chauffeur to come to see him. The summons could hardly have come at a worse moment, for Thomas was waiting for another visit from Mr Donaldson at which important decisions might be taken about the future. Reluctantly he left Sarah to receive Donaldson in his absence.

Thomas' interview with Mr Bellamy was short and sharp but could hardly have been called sweet. Both the men were already in a bad temper when it started.

'A suspicious character is seen coming to visit you and you won't say who it is,' Bellamy told Thomas. For what reason the 'character' had suddenly become 'suspicious' he didn't explain.

'Oh I'm beginning to see, sir,' Thomas replied hotly, 'you think me and Miss Roberts are in league together. She pinches it, gives it to me and I get rid of it through my underworld connections. Well, it's a plausible theory . . .'

'Don't be so damned impertinent,' said Bellamy with some reason. 'Look, I'm giving you every chance, Watkins . . .'

'And that's what I don't like,' Thomas replied quickly. 'If you'll pardon me saying so . . . that feeling of a need to justify myself when I consider there's no cause. I haven't been here long, like some I know, but I've done some good service. Handled a few difficult situations.'

Richard Bellamy was in no doubt the chauffeur was referring to the business of his wife's love letters.

'Earned myself a bit of credit,' Thomas went on, feeling he was gaining the upper hand, he decided to play the valued servant's hoary old trump card. 'But if you don't agree, then I think the best thing for all concerned is for me to give in my resignation.'

It won the trick and as usual Richard Bellamy was forced

to apologise; in exchange the chauffeur gave him the name of his visitor knowing full well that Mr Donaldson and his father were well known to Mr Bellamy and approved of by him.

'We share an interest in the latest type of motor cars, that is all,' Thomas explained.

When he got back to the garage the chauffeur found Sarah fending off his visitor for dear life.

'Let her go, will you,' he said with quiet menace. Mr Donaldson, who hadn't heard his host arrive, was surprised.

'Bit of a game, that's all,' said Donaldson forcing a laugh. 'Just a servant girl, isn't she? Fair game.'

A second later Thomas hit him hard in the stomach. The garage owner's son was tougher than he looked and the two men had a regular set to while Sarah watched enthralled. There was a certain amount of minor damage to the furniture and plenty of blood spilt before Donaldson staggered out of the garage clutching a bleeding face. Sarah fetched a bowl of water and bathed her hero's wounds. She felt just like the princess of the fairy tale and Thomas her true champion and parfait gentil knight.

Thomas Watkins had no such romantic notions. He had fought Donaldson because one of his possessions had been threatened and in his jungle it was the survival of the fittest that counted.

Richard Bellamy was having a bad day. The mystery of the missing brooch was no nearer to being solved and already he had had to withstand a furious attack from his wife for encouraging Mr Hudson to drive Miss Roberts into a state of hysteria. Unfortunately she had said some hard things about Miss Hodges and these being overheard by Lady Southwold had caused a major family row between mother and daughter, each defending her own dependant.

It had come to the stage when Lady Southwold had given orders for her bags to be packed as she was evidently no longer welcome in her daughter's house when a man arrived from Cartier's the jewellers, with a morocco case containing the missing diamond brooch.

It had apparently quite escaped Lady Southwold's memory that she had left it to have a diamond re-set and the jewellers in their tactful way, hadn't wished to bother her about it until after her husband's Memorial Service.

From such small beginnings are great storms born in teacups.

CHAPTER ELEVEN

Elizabeth Kirbridge soon found herself attacked again by her old enemy, boredom. The two weeks she had spent at Frinton with Nanny and Lucy had felt like two years and now that she was back in London she felt dull and lethargic and nothing in life seemed the least interesting. When her parents set off on their usual round of shooting house parties in Scotland and Yorkshire she did not accompany them, even less anxious to get involved in 'Society' than before her disastrous journey into married life.

One day early in August an old friend from the same finishing school in Dresden came to tea. Ellen Bouverie had changed from the pale, sensitive girl Elizabeth remembered. She was still pale but had an intense almost religious fervour about her. Ellen had become very involved in the Suffragette movement and it became clear that her prime motive in calling was to enlist Elizabeth into the ranks of the Women's Social and Political Union.

Elizabeth didn't really give a fig any more for women's rights but because it was something to do she went with Ellen to a few of the W.S.P.U. meetings all of which she found exceedingly tedious, many of the women who were there were like herself unhappy, frustrated and felt themselves misfits in life.

A mass attack on the houses of various members of the government had been planned and Ellen asked Elizabeth to be a member of her group. There was still a strong element of the tomboy in Elizabeth and the thought of hurling bricks through a few windows appealed to her sense of adventure.

The affair started splendidly, the windows were broken, the slogans were daubed and the infuriated junior minister even appeared in person accompanied by some guests who were dining with him; unfortunately so did the police and the ladies were taken off to spend the night in the cells.

The next day at the magistrate's court Elizabeth was told to her surprise that her fine of forty shillings had been paid by a gentleman and that she was free to go. Elizabeth's bene-factor was standing outside the court, tall and elegant and quizzical. Elizabeth read the card he presented to her: 'Mr Julius Karekin.' The card was properly engraved, that was all right, thought Elizabeth, but no club, that was suspicious. Even more suspicious was the fact that she clearly remembered smashing Mr Karekin's top hat the night before and he was the last person she could have expected to befriend her.

He had found her bag on the site of the fracas and from the evidence it contained had traced its charming owner. Very much on her guard Elizabeth accompanied Mr Karekin back in his chauffeur-driven Mercedes Benz motor car to his rooms in Albany to collect her property.

Karekin's rooms were alluring, furnished in a rich, refined rather flamboyant style. The cakes and the coffee were irre-sistible. In spite of her determination to keep Mr Karekin very much at arm's length, Elizabeth began to enjoy herself. Julius Karekin amused her, he was witty and endearingly frank. His father had been an Armenian carpet merchant and he himself was a financier, dealing in stocks in the City of London and very good at it indeed. It so happened that Elizabeth had been left a small legacy by an old great aunt the year before and because she saw in it the chance of financial independence it meant much to her. She mentioned the fact to Mr Karekin who said he would gladly advise her if she would show him her list of securities. The tea parties in the rooms in Albany began to become a weekly habit and Elizabeth found her legacy growing in the most amazing manner with the help of Julius Karekin's skilled manipulations. There was a withdrawn quality about her new friend that puzzled and attracted Elizabeth; he was polite, witty, charming but always the same.

'He'll want his pound of flesh one day, you'll see,' Rose warned Elizabeth. She was her only confidante and extremely suspicious of Mr Karekin and of her young mistress' sudden interest in money.

'I'd have thought you had enough of that already,' she remarked.

'No, Rose,' Elizabeth explained, 'not half enough. Not of my own. Without money I'll stay trapped here in the fond embrace of my family until I . . . just fade away into nothingness. I've got to escape.'

One day as Loris, Julius Karekin's manservant let her into the hall of the rooms in Albany a woman came out of the sitting room and gave Elizabeth such a look in passing that could looks kill she would have been killed stone dead on the spot. She swept out slamming the front door behind her.

'Another lady seeking advice,' Julius explained, as Loris poured out the champagne.

'You have a lot of ladies seeking advice?' Elizabeth asked lightly.

'Of course,' Julius admitted. 'There's safety in numbers, and I always try to please.'

'She didn't look very pleased to me,' said Elizabeth.

'Can you blame her?' Julius demanded, holding his glass up to her in a mock romantic gesture, 'your youthful beauty would make the moon herself pale with envy.'

The words were spoken in jest but later, as Elizabeth examined her face in her dressing table mirror, she remembered them again. It was the first time anyone had said she was beautiful for what seemed a very long time.

Apart from money Julius was extremely interested in the British political system; he knew every post any member of Elizabeth's family had held in the government back to the Conquest, far more than Elizabeth knew herself. His curiosity intrigued her.

'You seem to have studied the history of my family very carefully,' she said.

'I like to know the form before I place a bet,' Julius admitted with a smile. Something seemed to jump inside Elizabeth.

'Are you betting on me?'

She hadn't meant to ask quite such a leading question, so she laughed to show it was just a joke.

Julius Karekin laughed as well. 'I may,' he replied lightly. 'I have always found the combination of beauty and high birth very attractive.'

'Snob!'

'Of course. But what do you expect from the son of an Armenian carpet merchant?'

Elizabeth was quite disarmed.

'Do you know, Julius,' she said suddenly serious, 'I think

my parents might almost approve of you.' She turned to face him. 'Would you like to meet them?'

'I would like to meet them,' Julius admitted equally seriously, 'but they would not approve of me.'

'How do you know?'

'Because they would think as you thought when you first met me; they would think I was a dirty foreign Jew, my hands soiled with filthy lucre trying to ingratiate myself with them.'

Elizabeth nodded; what he said was very near to the truth.

'And they would be right,' Julius went on, 'except for the fact that I am not actually a Jew.' He shrugged his shoulders. 'And they would immediately jump to the conclusion that I had my cunning predatory eye on their daughter . . .'

'You are being absurd,' Elizabeth retorted, her words sounding less convincing than she would have liked.

'No I am not. They would be right again.' His eyes never left her face. 'That long upper lip; those grey green eyes; the way your hair grows off your forehead.' He touched her hair. 'I find them strangely disturbing.'

Elizabeth gave a forced gay laugh.

'Rose said you would want your pound of flesh.' She tried to make a joke of it.

Julius laughed. 'Rose, not without a thorn,' he replied, 'but percipient.'

He took her gently in his arms and kissed her on the lips and she didn't resist. After a moment she responded to his mouth.

'I have a daughter, Julius,' she said very quietly.

'Lots of married ladies have daughters.'

'She is not my husband's child. It was a mistake.'

Julius nodded to show he understood.

'We won't make any mistakes, Elizabeth,' he said almost in a whisper and she knew that she could trust him.

Almost as much as making money Julius Karekin liked making love to beautiful women. It could be said that he was a professional in both fields. In Elizabeth he found an eager willing pupil unspoilt by the bad habits learned from other men. If she had been quick to learn the skills of the stock exchange she was even quicker and more enthusiastic in learning the arts of Aphrodite. By morning Julius was beginning to wonder how he would ever manage to get through a full day's work in the City of London.

'Won't they begin to wonder?' he suggested tentatively.

'Who?' asked Elizabeth.

'Your parents,' Julius replied. 'Or do you often do this?'

'Pig!' she shouted. 'Armenian peasant!' and gave him a hard punch in the kidneys. It was something that Julius Karekin had never experienced before in his own bed.

'Rose will make it all right,' Elizabeth explained. 'Rose is a brick.'

Julius was intrigued. He had never found or expected such loyalty from servants.

'You really trust Rose?'

'I think she is the only person in the whole wide world I really do trust.'

She leant over and bit his ear.

Rose didn't let her down. When Mr Hudson complained that the kitchen had informed him that Miss Elizabeth's breakfast hadn't been touched, she lied nobly.

'She isn't feeling very peckish,' she said. 'Just a little upset.'

Mr Hudson passed the news on to the morning room. Said Lady Marjorie, 'Oh I must go up and see her. Perhaps she should see the doctor.'

'Rose also mentioned that Mrs Kirbridge was having a wee nap,' the butler explained.

'Well, that's the best cure there is . . .' They both smiled at this comfortable cliché. Rose had done her work well.

It wasn't until after ten-thirty that Julius Karekin was able to escape from the clutches of his insatiable Siren. Even then, as he struggled to dress himself without the help of his valet, she would have drawn him back to her.

'Come back to me,' she begged. 'Forget the dull old city for one day.'

'You don't seem to realise that the market is open already,' Julius replied as he fought with his cravat. 'I have missed one important meeting already, and the Kaffir Consols dividend is being declared at midday.'

Elizabeth jumped out of bed draping herself in the big fur that acted as a bedcover.

'I know,' she said with sudden inspiration. 'I will come to the City with you.'

Julius looked up to Heaven; this girl was capable of anything.

'One moment I will be a bear,' Elizabeth explained, 'growling and snarling and pulling down Consols and Foreign Rails and Breweries by the million with my sharp ruthless claws.'

She clawed and growled at Julius. 'The next I shall be a bull charging in among all those brokers and jobbers and stuffy old top hatters tossing portfolios of Equities and Industrials high in the air with one flick of my gilt-edged horns.'

Elizabeth dropped the fur rug and reached her arms out

towards her lover in a last desperate effort to tempt him to stay. Julius seized his morning coat and ran out of the room. Loris was outside with a welcome cup of coffee and a host of complaints. Most of his master's ladies came in the evening and stayed for an hour or two at the most but this young lady who stayed all night and half the morning! She was impossible! How could anyone run a household under such conditions? Julius was inclined to agree with Loris. During the day the matter occupied far more of his mind than such a trivial matter warranted.

'He laughed when I told him about you saying he'd want his pound of flesh,' Elizabeth told Rose, safely back in her own room.

'I'm sure he did. And not even your nightdress!' she clicked her teeth disapprovingly.

'I hate all nightdresses,' Elizabeth exclaimed. 'Let's burn the lot!'

Rose shook her head as Elizabeth looked at herself in the long mirror.

'I'm tingling all over with happiness,' she confessed to Rose, 'and I don't feel the teeniest prick of guilt or remorse . . . funny isn't it.'

Rose didn't find it funny, she found it shocking.

'I wonder why bodies are so important,' Elizabeth argued with herself. 'I wonder . . . I wonder if I'd known about it before. I wonder if Lawrence . . . ?'

She shrugged. No-one would ever know.

'He says that there can be no real love unless two bodies are joined together in perfect union,' she explained to Rose very seriously.

'Is that what you're going to tell your parents?' Rose asked in her sniffy voice.

'They mustn't know!' Elizabeth was horrified. 'And none of the other servants, Rose. Not that they could ever find out.'

'That's what her ladyship thought,' Rose replied in an unguarded moment, 'but we all knew.'

'What did you say, Rose?' Elizabeth asked with great interest.

'Nothing,' Rose answered backpedalling, 'it just slipped out.'

'Tell me Rose,' Elizabeth demanded going right up to her. 'Tell me. I've told you my secrets, now you must tell me yours!' She took both Rose's arms and refused to let her escape. Reluctantly Rose told what she knew of Lady Marjorie's love affair with Captain Hammond of the Khyber Rifles.

When Elizabeth came round to Julius Karekin's rooms that evening he didn't even allow her to take off her coat, but hustled her into his motor car and took her round to a small shop in a street in the middle of Mayfair.

When he had opened the door and lit the gaslamp Elizabeth saw that they were in a rather dusty old ladies hat shop. Julius explained that he had just bought it, complete with staff, as part of a property investment.

'Rather dull old hats,' said Elizabeth looking round.

'That's what I thought,' Julius replied.

'What's it called?' she asked.

'Whatever you like,' he answered.

Elizabeth's eyes opened wide. 'Whatever *I* like!'

'It's yours—if you want it.'

Elizabeth could hardly believe her ears. 'Of course I want it. I adore hats,' she said. 'I've always adored hats.'

She turned to Julius and hugged him like a little girl who has been given a birthday present.

'Oh Julius, I can't believe it!'

She kissed him passionately. Julius smiled. His plan had worked admirably.

'Paint it any colour you like,' he said. 'Choose whatever hats you like. Call it what you like.'

'You are a darling,' she exclaimed. 'I shall make it the smartest, chicest, Frenchest hat shop in London!'

She walked round the showroom thinking what she would do. Suddenly she had a moment of doubt.

'Is it really a present?' she asked.

Julius smiled and shrugged. 'Shall we say a loan?' he said.

Her parents received the news of the hat shop better than Elizabeth had expected.

'A hat shop, darling? How quite extraordinary,' said Lady Marjorie.

'It sounds rather fun,' Richard Bellamy admitted. 'Whatever gave you the idea?'

'I happened to meet someone who offered me the job,' Elizabeth replied with careful casual vagueness, 'and I do need something to do.'

That was a fact that her parents could hardly deny.

Elizabeth told them all about the shop and her plans for it and she even asked them to help her to find a name for it.

'Darling, I really can't think what to call it,' said Lady Marjorie. 'I've never had to name a hat shop.'

'What about "Paris Modes"?' Richard suggested.

'No, it must be "Madame" something,' Elizabeth explained. 'They always are.'

Richard suggested 'Madame Yvonne'. It had a nice French ring to it. Elizabeth seemed to approve.

'I know what made you think of that,' Lady Marjorie said to her husband and turned to Elizabeth. 'When I first met your father in Paris he had a rather dreadful common girl friend called Yvonne.'

'She was the daughter of a Minister,' Richard said defensively.

'She was still common,' Lady Marjorie insisted, 'and had dyed hair.'

'I admit I did better,' Richard agreed complacently.

'I should hope so,' his wife replied.

'Father's dreadful common girl friend shall be immortalised,' said Elizabeth. 'Madame Yvonne it shall be.'

And Madame Yvonne it was.

Elizabeth inherited two pretty young salesgirls, an adequate cashier and a very competent manageress and head saleswoman called Mademoiselle Jeanette. Mademoiselle, as she was always called, was a rather worn professional milliner from Peckham who had been in the trade since she was fourteen and knew all there was to know. As Elizabeth was a lady she didn't resent her presence in the least and was pleased to teach her some of the tricks of the trade.

Elizabeth learnt that although all the hats must appear to have come from Paris it was pointless and extravagant to buy them in France as they could be copied in London just as well; she learned that the customer is always right and that the greatest compliment, only reserved for the richest and the most distinguished, was for Elizabeth in her guise of Madame

Yvonne to tie the veil herself; she learnt that although the salesgirls and Mademoiselle always adopted a French accent when in the showroom, Madame Yvonne must never do so and that there were certain ladies of quality, many of them famous names in Society, who never paid their bills however rich they were. In fact Elizabeth learnt a great many detrimental facts about her own sex that she had never so much as suspected before.

She herself supervised the insertion of advertisements in the ladies' magazines and was rewarded by flattering articles by the fashion editors in the same magazines. Soon ladies of all sorts came flocking to the new shop and the hats themselves started selling like hot cakes.

Every evening at closing time Julius called for Elizabeth and took her back to supper in his rooms. He took elaborate care to see that they were never seen together in public and Elizabeth was always delivered back to the corner of Eaton Place by midnight or thereabouts. Experience should have told Elizabeth that this state of bliss was too good to last.

One morning Mademoiselle came into the office and pointed out a customer who had just come into the showroom.

'Mrs Descort,' said Mademoiselle, 'she's been sued by every milliner in London. Owes hundreds. My last place we took her to court and were granted judgement but we never saw a penny—never will.'

Elizabeth nodded; she was uncomfortably aware that she had seen Mrs Descort somewhere before.

'Whatever happens she mustn't be given credit,' Mademoiselle warned Elizabeth and returned to do battle while Elizabeth hovered rather uneasily in the background waiting for her cue.

'This one is really too hideous,' Mrs Descort remarked, pushing an orange confection to one side, 'but I'll take this one,' she pointed to the hat that she was wearing, 'and these other four. Kindly send them round to my address; you know it, I think, Mademoiselle.'

'I'm afraid that this establishment does not allow credit, Madame,' Mademoiselle explained firmly.

'And who is in charge of this establishment?' Mrs Descort demanded brusquely.

'Madame Yvonne,' said Mademoiselle and Elizabeth knew it was her turn. When she faced Mrs Descort she remembered. It was the woman who had passed her in Julius Karekin's hall. Her predecessor, as she suspected with some reason, in Julius Karekin's bed.

'I am informed that you don't give customers credit?' Mrs Descort said in an icy voice.

'That is correct, Madam,' Elizabeth's reply was polite.

'Then soon you will have no customers,' Mrs Descort told her. 'As I happen to know who owns this shop, I think an exception can be made.'

'I am in charge, and I am sorry that I cannot give you credit, Madam,' Elizabeth replied, and gained an approving nod from Mademoiselle.

Mrs Descort stood up. 'Aren't you the Bellamy girl?' she asked at the door.

'Yes, Madam.'

Mrs Descort drew her sables round her and swept out still wearing the new hat. Elizabeth ran after her but was restrained by Mademoiselle.

'Her old one had nine feathers,' Mademoiselle held up

Mrs Descort's abandoned hat. 'Properly dressed they're worth far more than the one she's taken.'

The salesgirls were delighted but for Elizabeth the victory had a bitter taste.

As he returned from Westminster, Richard Bellamy saw a strange woman in a fur coat come out of his house and hail a taxi. It struck him as odd that a lady should demean herself in such a way.

'Who was your visitor?' he asked his wife when he had joined her for tea in the morning room.

'A woman called Mrs Descort,' Lady Marjorie answered in a distrait voice. Richard frowned. They hardly knew the Descorts beyond a nodding acquaintance; they were doubtful people of no account.

'She came to tell me that Elizabeth is living with a man called Julius Karekin,' Lady Marjorie said in a dangerously steady voice.

For a moment her husband didn't answer. 'Do you think it's true?' he asked. 'She's a dreadful gossip, I believe.'

'Why should she bother to lie about it?'

Richard Bellamy shrugged unhappily. 'I don't know,' he admitted, 'and I've heard the Descorts have been running this Karekin fellow for all they were worth. They haven't a bean of their own of course.'

'I gather he's quite beyond the pale,' Lady Marjorie went on, 'a foreign commerçant straight from the gutter,' she sighed unhappily. 'I imagine there's been some sort of bust up with this woman . . .'

'I suppose it's bound to get around.'

'If you hired a town crier you wouldn't do better than Margot Descort,' Lady Marjorie assured him.

It was six o'clock on a cold blustery February night when the Rolls Royce pulled up outside Madame Yvonne. The shop was just closing and Elizabeth was in the office entering the day's sales in the ledger.

'Mother darling, how lovely to see you,' she said, turning up the gas in the showroom. 'Let me show you everything.'

Lady Marjorie looked round. 'Elizabeth,' she asked, 'who does this shop belong to?' And Elizabeth knew that Mrs Descort had set about her work with despatch. She took a deep breath and determined to keep her temper.

'This shop belongs to Mr Julius Karekin,' she said, 'and I am his mistress or as Mrs Descort may have put it "his kept woman", as she was before me. Because you don't know him you think he is a common little upstart and dishonest at that. Because I know him I can tell you that he is funny, intelligent and generous and as much a gentleman as any of your friends —and I have never been so happy in all my life.'

Lady Marjorie realised she had a hard task ahead.

'Don't you see he's nothing but a climber?' she told her daughter. 'He's using you.'

'Of course he's using me,' Elizabeth admitted, 'and I am using him. We are very frank about it.'

'You could never marry him, darling.'

'No,' Elizabeth agreed. 'That's a definite asset in both our eyes.'

Lady Marjorie went through to the office and warmed her hands at the fire.

'Don't you see what damage it will do?' she said.

'You mean to you. To the family escutcheon,' Elizabeth began to get angry in spite of herself. 'I should have thought that after all my previous misdemeanours there was hardly a square inch left for me to blot—or is it dent?'

Lady Marjorie knew that it was useless to tell her daughter that she was making herself an outcast from Society. Elizabeth wouldn't care a jot.

'But darling, if you ever wanted to get married again,' she tried.

'But I'm unmarriageable, that's just it,' Elizabeth said wearily. 'By an unfortunate accident I have a child by another man and my husband knows it. While we keep his mouth shut with a comfortable pension do you think Lawrence is going to give me grounds for divorce?'

Lady Marjorie could hardly deny her reasoning.

'Don't you see, mother, I'm trapped,' Elizabeth went on. 'Do you want me to sit at home for ever and wither away till I'm a bitter old maid, like Princess Victoria.'

The Queen's treatment of her daughter was well known and one of her least endearing characteristics.

'It's all so unfair,' Elizabeth sighed. 'If I was a man it wouldn't matter a bit. Uncle Hugo's spent his whole life seducing every woman in sight and everyone thinks he's a hell of a fellow and I get pilloried because I go to bed with a man I happen to like very much.'

Elizabeth very exactly described the conventional morals of the Edwardian aristocracy.

'You should try to discipline yourself, hundreds of women are in the same position as yourself.'

Elizabeth ignored this well-used cliché. 'You are so much

more beautiful than I am—and more attractive,' she said. 'Haven't you ever had an . . . an infatuation?'

'I've never given into a mere indulgence,' Lady Marjorie replied, never suspecting a trap.

'Was Captain Hammond not a mere indulgence?'

The question hit Lady Marjorie so hard because it was so unexpected. Until that moment she hadn't the least idea that anyone else had an inkling of her relationship with Charles Hammond.

Elizabeth was amazed to find that she was feeling sorry for her mother.

'You see we're the same sort of people really,' she said quietly. Lady Marjorie shrugged in distress.

'I am not very proud of my friendship with Charles Hammond,' she admitted. 'I stopped in time. I realised what a lot I stood to lose.'

'I have nothing to lose that I care about.'

'I never let it become a scandal. I stuck to the rules.'

'Your rules,' Elizabeth was scornful. 'What hypocrisy! As long as no one knows about it, it's all right!'

Lady Marjorie smiled sadly, remembering that Charles had used exactly the same words. They would have liked each other, Elizabeth and her dear, dead Charles.

'You were lucky to have such loyal servants and such a devoted husband,' Elizabeth continued, determined to rub it in.

Lady Marjorie looked up in a sudden alarm. 'Your father didn't know about it. He must never know.'

'I won't tell him,' Elizabeth promised. 'But I bet he did know. Father's deep and he doesn't miss much.'

They both knew this to be the truth.

'But he'd never do anything to hurt you.'

Lady Marjorie turned away, more upset than she wished to show. After a moment she made a last plea to her daughter to come home.

'If you will receive Julius.'

'Not under any circumstances. It wouldn't do.'

They were the same sort of people.

Sir Geoffrey Dillon, the family solicitor, was the appointed executor of old Lord Southwold's will. Hugo, Lady Marjorie's younger brother who succeeded to the title and the estate, was a wild and extravagant man who had accumulated huge debts over the years and spent most of his time abroad. It was one of the provisions of the old earl's will that these debts should be paid off by the estate on his son inheriting the title.

'I have to find just over a hundred thousand pounds in cash,' Sir Geoffrey told Lady Marjorie and Richard. 'Quickly and in cash. There are seventeen leasehold properties all here in Westminster purchased by your father, Lady Marjorie.' He looked briefly at his papers. 'And not within the entail. I am forced to put them on the market immediately. This house is among them.'

Lady Marjorie couldn't believe it. Her father would never have allowed such a thing to happen to her if he were still alive. But old Lord Southwold was dead and Hugo was somewhere in the wilds of Canada and didn't give a damn how much he inconvenienced his sister.

'Naturally you will be offered the first refusal on the purchase of the lease,' Sir Geoffrey assured her. 'It should attract some six thousand pounds on the open market.'

Richard Bellamy was put into what seemed to be a ludicrous

position. Six thousand pounds didn't sound a great deal of money but he himself had very little capital and received no salary at all for his services as a Member of Parliament.

Lady Marjorie's income from her marriage settlement was substantial but no more than adequate for her standard of living. The capital was settled on the children so that there was no money available which was not entailed or in trust. Richard went to the city and consulted his banker and his stockbroker; he was advised that the terms on which he could borrow the money would be ruinous. In a way Richard was pleased. He disliked his brother-in-law and thought he was behaving very badly to his sister: it irked him to have to borrow money to pay off such a worthless man's debts. He told his wife that they would have to leave Eaton Place and find somewhere more economical to live.

Already deeply distressed by Elizabeth's behaviour, this new blow left Lady Marjorie numb and at a loss.

'Is it absolutely necessary to move, Richard?' she asked. Like most women of her generation she had little idea of finance and trusted her husband implicitly in such matters.

'I'm afraid it is,' Richard assured her.

'Where?' she asked rather despairingly.

'There are some very nice squares in Paddington,' her husband suggested as brightly as he could.

'No, Richard,' Lady Marjorie was quite definite. 'Not north of the Park.'

'Well, what about Chelsea?'

'Only hooligans and artists live in Chelsea,' she said.

'Kensington?' Richard queried. Lady Marjorie considered the qualities of Kensington. 'I had a governess once who lived in Kensington.' It seemed the last word on the subject.

'How depressing,' she said.

The bad news soon found its way below stairs as bad news always does. Like their betters upstairs, the servants were at first incredulous that such a disaster could ever happen to them, but when certain straws in the wind told them that it was indeed the truth they became fearful. An air of depression settled on 165 Eaton Place both upstairs and downstairs.

Julius Karekin was cross with Elizabeth for breaking with her mother. It didn't suit his plans at all.

'But if you'd heard the things she said about you,' Elizabeth was indignant, 'and she doesn't even know you.'

'It's quite usual,' Julius told her, 'and quite understandable.'

'Well it shouldn't be,' Elizabeth snapped, 'and don't be so . . . so reasonable.'

'But I am reasonable,' he said and tried to explain. 'People like your mother, all her class of person, are frightened and a little jealous of us.' Elizabeth failed to see why. 'They see us as a threat to what Lord Northcliffe's young men are pleased to call the Bastions of Privilege. Our success in commerce is beginning to give us an influence in the running of this country. They see it as a threat to their absolute power over government, over society, over something that they have come to regard as theirs, absolutely, by some divine right.' He smiled at her. 'That's why they have to pretend that anyone who works in commerce and makes money must be unclean and untouchable. They don't really believe it, of course, but it is a sort of way of protecting their bastions.'

'It's all nonsense,' said Elizabeth crossly.

'Of course,' Julius agreed with maddening reasonableness.

When they were still talking Rose arrived post haste from

Eaton Place with the news that Elizabeth's parents were on the move.

'They've been looking at houses in Kensington all the morning. Thomas took them in the motor, so he should know,' said Rose. 'And Mr Hudson's given us a lecture about tightening our belts and wasting not and wanting not and weathering the storm. And I may be going to lose my housemaid . . . and Mr Watkins is worried they'll sell the Rolls Royce . . . and Mrs Bridges is in a proper state because she's had her cream cut to two pints a day and she's talking about retirement and boarding houses in Brighton.'

There was no doubt the crisis was a real one.

'I think you ought to come home, Miss Elizabeth,' said Rose, and Elizabeth agreed with her.

The next day Julius Karekin went to see Sir Geoffrey Dillon on business of his own.

A week later the solicitor returned to Eaton Place to ask the Bellamys if they wished to purchase the remaining years of the lease. They told him regretfully that they were unable to do so.

'In that case I have a purchaser,' said Sir Geoffrey. Lady Marjorie looked up angrily; the solicitor seemed to be acting with an almost indecent haste. 'A very good property, at a very good price,' Sir Geoffrey assured her complacently. 'Soon snapped up.'

'Sir Geoffrey,' Lady Marjorie asked tentatively, 'when will we have to . . . to . . . give. . . .'

She couldn't think of the word.

'Vacant possession?' Sir Geoffrey suggested helpfully and Lady Marjorie nodded.

A look came over Sir Geoffrey's face which in another less serious and important person might have been described as 'puckish'.

'I'm not sure that will be necessary now,' he said.

Richard Bellamy was not amused.

'What on earth do you mean?' he demanded.

'I took the liberty of bringing the prospective purchaser with me,' Sir Geoffrey said as innocently as he was able and Elizabeth burst into the room.

'I was earwigging at the keyhole,' she said. 'It's me.'

Lady Marjorie and Richard Bellamy listened in dazed silence as Sir Geoffrey explained that a certain Mr Julius Karekin had made him an offer for the property which he felt bound to accept in the circumstances. He added that the same Mr Julius Karekin had already put down a deposit on the house and was ready to complete, and furthermore the same Mr Julius Karekin had asked him to prepare a deed of gift assigning the lease to Mrs Lawrence Kirbridge.

'And I'm going to give it to you,' Elizabeth told them. 'I know how much you love the house and so do I and so does James . . . and after all the money you've spent on me and little Lucy, it's the least I can do to try to repay you.'

Lady Marjorie thought it over. She was a proud and obstinate woman not at all used to changing her mind; to her, Elizabeth's offer, engineered by Karekin, seemed nothing more than accepting a bribe from the enemy. It took all her husband's powers of persuasion to convince her that it was unfair and unreasonable to both her family and herself to refuse the offer.

'What sort of man is this Karekin?' Lady Marjorie asked Sir Geoffrey.

'Very agreeable,' Sir Geoffrey assured her; Karekin was after all his client, 'and very able I'm told; one of the most able new men in the City of London, and fast becoming a very rich one.'

'Evidently you got on with him all right?' said Richard.

'My dear Richard,' Sir Geoffrey replied, 'in my profession it is most unwise not to make a point of getting on with very rich, able men . . . and if I may say so,' and here he addressed them both, 'he's the sort of man who might be very useful to the Conservative Party in the future . . . very useful.'

Below stairs the news was received with a mixture of delighted astonishment tinged with disapproval.

'I must say I find it very peculiar, very peculiar indeed,' said Mr Hudson. 'Still it's not our place to question the family's financial arrangements. We should thank God for small blessings.'

'Small blessings!' Rose exclaimed. 'This is a great, big, enormous blessing.'

Rose echoed the general sentiment in the servants' hall although Mrs Bridges had doubts about the benefactor.

'Put a turban on his head and he'd be out of the Arabian Nights,' she said.

'I think you will find that Mr Karekin is an Armenian gentleman, Mrs Bridges, not an Arabian,' Mr Hudson suggested. Mrs Bridges remained unrepentant.

'They're all the same,' she grumbled. 'Coffee coloured with oily hair and rings on their fingers.'

'And bells on their toes,' said the footman.

'And bells to answer, Edward,' said Mr Hudson.

Elizabeth and Julius Karekin were coming to tea.

CHAPTER TWELVE

'There's a lesson for you,' Sarah said to little Lucy. 'Don't you eat two helpings of Mrs Bridges' plum pudding when you grow up into a big girl.'

As it was Christmas she put her queasy feeling down to eating too much. In the new year Sarah realised that it wasn't Mrs Bridges' plum pudding at all. She was pregnant. It wasn't until the end of January that she summoned up the courage to tell Thomas Watkins about it.

'We'll have to see then, won't we?' was all he said hardly looking up from his motoring magazine. Sarah was so relieved that he wasn't angry that she hardly realised that his casual attitude was more dangerous.

'You'll have to think up a story won't you?' he said after a few minutes. 'I'll give you story, Thomas Watkins,' she replied, and that was all that was said.

Sarah tried not to think about the baby growing inside her; and because she was so busy with Lucy and the nursery and had a natural talent for living from minute to minute she was able to put off the evil day until early in March.

Mrs Bridges noticed there were two pieces of cut cake missing from the tin in the servants' hall and naturally she blamed Ruby. It wasn't till Sarah had a dizzy fit and dropped the nursery tray and Mrs Bridges remembered the way she'd finished off the cold toad-in-the-hole the day before that she put two and two together.

'You know what I think, Sarah,' she told the nursery maid when she'd sent the junior servants out of the way, 'I think you're eating for two. Am I right?' It was an unhappy chance that Mr Hudson came into the servants' hall before Sarah could reply. He always had an uncanny knack of being in the right place when there was any trouble.

The two of them sat down and looked at Sarah carefully until she became uneasily aware of her thickening body.

'Sarah,' Mr Hudson demanded. 'Are you or are you not expecting? I require a simple answer.'

'What if I am?' Sarah gave herself away in four words.

'There, I told you,' Mrs Bridges was triumphantly proud of her discovery.

'I'm shocked,' Mr Hudson said, suiting his tone to his words, 'shocked to my very fibre.'

'It weren't my fault,' Sarah pleaded.

'The cry of the hussy,' Mrs Bridges exclaimed. 'You're talking to me and Mr Hudson, girl. We know you don't get babies smelling the flowers.'

She made excuses, she pleaded with them for mercy, she wailed and she moaned but they were not having any of it. Sarah had cried wolf several times too often, and their hearts were hardened.

'Who is the father?' Mr Hudson demanded. 'What manner of person?'

'What manner of person?' said Sarah playing for time. On her way up and down to the park with the baby in her perambulator Sarah had invented many different stories for use in this very predicament. Now she wondered which one was most likely to be believed.

'Well, he was . . . er . . . it wasn't my fault. It was Nanny's afternoon off and I slipped out you see . . .'

All the stories started like that; she decided to go on with the one about the toff in the Burlington Arcade; it was her favourite. A complicated series of incidents while in search of gripe water for the baby's wind had left her stranded in the pouring rain in Piccadilly and forced her to seek shelter in the Burlington Arcade.

'It poured stair-rods,' she explained. 'Really came down in buckets.'

She looked anxiously for signs of belief in the two faces. They were still reserving their judgement.

'There was this man you see,' Sarah went on.

'In the arcade,' said Mrs Bridges.

'That's right,' Sarah agreed, pleased that Mrs Bridges was following. 'He was sheltering too.'

'What sort of man?' Mr Hudson asked.

'Well . . .' Sarah explained. 'Oh, a toff. A real gent. He had a silk hat and a silk brolly and . . . er . . . not too young. But not old. The sort anyone'd trust.' She gave Mr Hudson a sad smile. 'Tall and distinguished and—he had bits of silver hair at the sides—'

She paused, 'and his coat had a baby lamb collar,' she added, with that fatal addiction to corroborative detail, intended to give artistic verisimilitude to an otherwise bald and unconvincing narrative, but which always had the opposite effect when it came from Sarah's lips.

Mrs Bridges looked at Mr Hudson. 'If this distinguished looking man possessed a hat and an umbrella, why was he sheltering from the rain?' he asked.

'Exactly,' said Mrs Bridges meaningfully.

'Well, he was waiting for a hackney,' Sarah said quickly. 'No, I tell a lie. It was a carriage. *His* carriage. He was waiting for his own carriage.'

The distinguished man with the baby lamb collar had offered her a lift back and on the way they had stopped at his rooms. Sarah wasn't sure where they were, it might have been Eaton Place.

'Or High Street, China,' Mrs Bridges added drily.

The man had offered her some brandy because she was so cold and then when she was a bit tiddly not being used to strong liquor he had taken terrible advantage of the poor, innocent, little servant girl.

They heard her out not believing a word but curiously fascinated by the richness of the invention.

'She'll have to be told as soon as she gets back,' said Mrs Bridges definitely. Lady Marjorie was spending ten days in Biarritz with the old dowager, Lady Southwold.

Mr Hudson decided it was urgent and important enough for Mr Bellamy's ears. Mrs Bridges didn't agree.

'Servants in child is for women to talk about,' she told the butler. 'And discipline is for men to talk about, Mrs Bridges,' he answered, neatly putting the cook in her place.

Richard Bellamy was dismayed by the news and was inclined to take Mrs Bridges' view and wait for his wife's return. He counselled Mr Hudson to keep the information from the other servants. It was a pious hope. Mrs Bridges, who couldn't keep a secret for toffee, was already confiding in her friend, the chauffeur.

When Sarah came back from the park and rushed across to the garage to talk to Thomas, he was forewarned and forearmed. He had cut out an advertisement from a newspaper about a garage for sale in Kilburn for five hundred pounds and was reading it with great concentration.

'My Bible,' he told Sarah, showing her the piece of paper. 'The parable of the servant who dreamed of leaving his master and going out in the world to seek his own fortune . . . and it came to pass there was a small motor business for sale in Watford Lane, Kilburn . . .'

'Well you can forget it,' Sarah told him and poured out the whole story of the morning while Thomas did his best to pretend he was hearing it all for the first time.

'Now the cat's out of the bag, what are you going to do about me?' she demanded.

'Nothing,' said the chauffeur and walked over to the motor car and lifted the bonnet.

'Nothing!' Sarah's squeak was a mixture of outrage and fear. 'You got to do something, Tom. You've got to get another job and marry me and make it all respectable. I'm not going through all that again.'

Thomas was busy removing one of the sparking plugs from the engine. Sarah seized his arm and shouted at him.

'You'll have to look after me, Thomas, you can't leave me all alone to have my baby on the streets.'

He held up the plug to the light inspecting it very carefully.

'Tom, please,' Sarah pleaded.

'Go away. Go away, Sarah. I'm busy,' he said without looking at her.

'Busy,' she screamed, clawing at him. 'You get bleeding busy with me. I'll tell them. I'll tell them it was you!'

Thomas Watkins looked at her.

'They won't believe you will they?' he said very cool and

collected. 'Not after you've told them all about this fancy gent in the rain. With a baby fur collar was it?'

Sarah saw the trap she had fallen into.

'Oh my God, Tom!' she exclaimed, putting her hand over her mouth. He went over and began to clean the plug on the emery wheel thus drowning all Sarah's pleas for help.

He needed time to think.

Richard Bellamy always enjoyed spending a day alone at home undisturbed to prepare his speeches for the House of Commons. In addition he had received a cablegram from his son James containing the welcome news that he would be home from India for good in April. He was in a good mood when his chauffeur came to see him after luncheon. When Thomas Watkins asked his permission to take Sarah's hand in marriage he was surprised but not in any way dismayed.

'I'd like to help her out; make her respectable, see, sir,' Thomas explained.

'Marriage is a serious step,' Mr Bellamy counselled.

'Oh yes, sir,' Thomas's tone was deadly serious. 'Specially me being chapel. It's for life being chapel.'

'Marriage should be for life whatever you are,' said Mr Bellamy. For some moments he considered the chauffeur's proposition. The more he thought about it the better the idea became. It would mean that Sarah would be out of the way under the benign influence of a sensible, reliable man and at the same time they would all be relieved of a considerable weight on their consciences.

'Well Watkins, if you will marry Sarah, keep her out of mischief, look after her, I don't think you will find us ungrateful. It would solve what has become of late a very difficult family problem.'

'That thought was uppermost in my mind.'

'You really are the most exceptional man, Watkins.' Mr Bellamy was open in his admiration.

'Thank you, sir,' Watkins replied looking down at his hands. 'Naturally I shall do everything I can to make Sarah happy, sir, as far as my modest wages will allow.'

In such a cordial atmosphere it was most unlikely that two reasonable men of goodwill would fall out over the question of money and it was mutually agreed that in exchange for Thomas' unselfish act he should be rewarded with some new furniture and curtains for his flat above the garage and a wedding present which would take the form of money, a substantial sum of money.

It was hardly the moment to go into exact and vulgar details, but Thomas left the room believing that the garage in Kilburn was a very much more likely prospect than it had been ten minutes before.

Sarah was so overwhelmed with joy when she heard the news that Nanny had to give her a sedative. At first the other servants were numb with surprise. By supper time they were taking sides.

'What makes a good, honest young man with a chance to get on in life throw himself away on a creature like that is beyond me,' said Mrs Bridges. Mr Hudson was determined to be fair.

'Mr Watkins' gesture is noble. I confess it took me by surprise,' he announced. 'However it appears there is good in the most unlikely people.'

Rose disappeared into the sewing room in a sulk; she

wasn't talking to Sarah or Thomas Watkins and the sooner they got out of her life the better. She had a new underhouse parlourmaid called Daisy to train and she took it out on her.

Edward and Ruby kept their own counsel. They knew very well why Thomas was marrying Sarah.

When Lady Marjorie arrived home from abroad her husband was still at the House of Commons; her first thought when she read James' cable was that Sarah must be got rid of before her son reached London. Thus it was from Sarah's own lips that she first heard the story of the baby and the chauffeur's proposal.

'So you see, m'lady,' Sarah concluded her tale, 'it's going to be all right, isn't it?'

'No Sarah,' Lady Marjorie replied firmly. 'It is not going to be all right. Not by a long way.'

Sarah had already deduced from Lady Marjorie's frigid expression that she didn't altogether approve of her husband's arrangement.

'But m'lady. Mr Watkins . . .' Sarah began.

'Watkins is the chauffeur here,' Lady Marjorie interrupted, 'and you, in spite of very considerate treatment you have received from us, are once again expecting a child—this time as the result of some undesirable adventure on your afternoon off.'

Sarah bit her lip, wishing she could tell the mouldy old cow the truth. Lady Marjorie rang the bell for the butler.

'We can no longer take the responsibility for you, and I am certainly not going to allow a young man like Watkins to ruin his future career for some foolish act of misplaced chivalry,' said Lady Marjorie.

Mr Hudson came into the room. He had been waiting in the hall suspecting that there might be trouble.

'Hudson, will you inform Nanny that Sarah is leaving at once; as soon as she has had her dinner and packed her trunk.'

'Yes, m'lady,' Hudson replied rather shakily.

'But, m'lady . . .' Sarah almost shouted.

Lady Marjorie told the butler to send for Watkins and to remove the nursery maid.

Downstairs Sarah went round and round the servants' hall in an orgy of fury.

'The old bitch . . . rotten, raddled, old bitch! She can't stop us! She can't, she can't, she can't!'

'Don't you dare speak of your mistress like that,' Mr Hudson commanded.

'I speak as I find,' Sarah shouted. 'She's an old bitch!'

'It's the bad blood coming out,' Mrs Bridges nodded her head sagely.

'You'll see! He will marry me! She can't stop us.' Sarah was near to weeping.

'I think you'll find different,' Mr Hudson promised her grimly.

'Her ladyship?' said Mrs Bridges. 'Why she can twist Thomas Watkins round her little finger!'

Lady Marjorie was finding that seemingly simple act exceedingly difficult. Watkins was proving unusually stupid and obstinate. She tried flattery and cajolery, she pointed out the folly of marrying a wastrel like Sarah but still the chauffeur held out.

'As a man of honour and strictly brought up, I couldn't

go against my word,' he explained. 'You wouldn't expect me to, would you, m'lady? Not to go back on my word?'

Lady Marjorie looked at him.

'Are you absolutely determined to marry Sarah?' she asked in a dangerously calm voice. 'At all costs?'

'I am, m'lady,' Thomas replied with great sincerity, feeling that victory was near.

'I see,' Lady Marjorie said with something like a sigh. 'Well, that's very sad news.'

Thomas Watkins looked up quickly, not liking the sound of things.

'I was hoping perhaps that you'd have the sense to put your career first,' she went on. 'But I see now that it means nothing to you. So that's that. I can't force you to stay here against your will.'

She told him that he should pack immediately and take Sarah with him and that they would both be given a month's wages.

'That will be all, Watkins,' she said.

The chauffeur was so dumbfounded that he couldn't think of a word to say as he went out. He paused in the hall wondering what had gone wrong. He couldn't know it but he had no idea of the lengths to which Lady Marjorie would go to protect her beloved only son from further damage. For his sake she would happily have dismissed the whole staff then and there.

As Thomas walked slowly back to his garage he realised that the carefully built up edifice of his fine future was lying around him in ruins. The garage in Kilburn might as well have been in Bombay for all he would ever see of it. Being a man always cool in a crisis he sat down in his work room to plan a counter attack.

When Richard Bellamy returned from the house with the plaudits of his own front bench still ringing in his ears, anticipating a happy reunion with his beloved wife, he was considerably peeved to find that she had reversed all his domestic decisions in the short time that she had been home.

'I wish you wouldn't go against me, Marjorie,' he complained. 'It makes a man look such a damn fool when he says one thing and his wife says another.'

'Your wife *had* to say it,' Lady Marjorie retorted, 'because you were wrong.'

'To you I am invariably wrong,' Richard began angrily. 'Why am I wrong?'

'Because it is impossible to contemplate those two married and living under this roof.'

He took a little persuading but eventually was drawn round to the logic of his wife's argument.

'At least we can get rid of Sarah now with a clear conscience,' she told him. 'She won't starve.'

It seemed a little hard to Richard but he saw the sense of it.

'Perhaps it's for the best,' he said.

'I'm sure it is,' Lady Marjorie replied quite definitely. 'And in future, Richard, I beg you not to involve yourself in matters concerning the servants and running the house, while I am away.'

Before Richard could reply, the butler came in with a request from Thomas Watkins for a further interview.

'If he's simply going to argue for Sarah to stay on here as his wife,' Lady Marjorie said, 'there's no point in further discussion.'

'I expect he's come to say good-bye,' said Richard reasonably. 'I should like to say good-bye to him and thank him for his good service.'

Lady Marjorie pursed her lips.

'Ask him to come in, Hudson,' said her husband boldly.

Thomas Watkins wasn't so foolish as to try to cover the same ground that had proved so treacherous earlier in the day. This time he came humbly, cap in hand, to tell Lady Marjorie how sorry he was if he had seemed surly and ungracious earlier in the day. And he had good news for everyone, especially for himself and Sarah.

It seemed that on his making some enquiries in the mews by a happy chance there was a titled lady and gentleman living in Chester Square who had an old chauffeur giving up and were on the look out for just such a person as Thomas Watkins. Furthermore there was a nice flat above the garage, newly done up, and no objection to a married man.

'I'd just like to thank you m'lady, from both of us, for all the experience you have given us—we've learnt quite a lot of things since we've been in your employ, m'lady, in this house, and the knowledge we have gained should serve us in good stead in another household.'

He allowed a short pause for the import of all this to sink in.

'It was only to say not to worry about me and Sarah,' he went on humbly, 'we're fixed up all right, you see, with good prospects. Thank you, m'lady. Thank you, sir.' He made a little bow and departed.

As soon as the door was closed Lady Marjorie stood up with her eyes flashing.

'That was a threat. A direct threat!' she exclaimed. 'Isn't

it marvellous. One might have known. All that bowing and scraping and charm, then the minute they leave you all loyalty goes to the wind.'

It was the perennial cry of the betrayed mistress.

'I don't know what you're talking about,' said Richard. 'I didn't hear any threat.'

'Richard, I sometimes think you shut your eyes to things on purpose,' Lady Marjorie complained.

Sarah and Thomas knew all the secrets of the Bellamy family; they knew of James' unfortunate liaison; of Elizabeth's baby; of Lady Marjorie's affair with Captain Hammond, although Lady Marjorie naturally didn't bring this example into her argument. No doubt they would take great delight in spreading this gossip round the titled lady and gentleman's establishment in Chester Square. Soon it would be common knowledge in every servants' hall and consequently in every drawing room in London.

'Those two creatures are not in any circumstances to go to Chester Square as chauffeur and wife.'

'How can you stop them?' Richard asked reasonably.

'I can refuse them references.'

'If he's malicious as you say he is,' Richard argued, 'he'll tell the new people why you wouldn't give him a character and that'll make an even worse scandal.'

'Then you must think of something else,' Lady Marjorie raged. 'Do something, Richard!'

Richard Bellamy threw up his hands.

'Me?' he said. 'I thought you said all matters involving the servants were your affair.'

'You got us into this mess in the first place,' she replied. 'Now you can get us out of it. It's all your fault.'

Richard Bellamy had had a long and tiring day.

'Oh damn servants,' he said. 'Why in God's name does one have to put up with them!'

'And wives too,' he might have added and been forgiven. But he was a man and a husband and he accepted the fact that wives, being of the frail and weaker sex are privileged to fall back on arguments that are not always strictly logical.

Richard Bellamy had not been trained as a diplomat for nothing. He called a truce or rather an interregnum during which neither party should make any further advances until they had slept on it. When the chauffeur had taken Lady Marjorie to a ladies reception that evening in the Rolls Royce, Richard took the opportunity to have a look round the garage and the workroom. He noticed with interest that several advertisements had been cut out of local newspapers and one especially had been encircled with a red pencilled line. It gave him food for profitable thought.

The next morning he paid another visit to the garage. There were evident signs of packing going on and Thomas Watkins was rather obviously busy. Richard touched on the motor car and its needs before leading the conversation by way of the whole new motoring industry to the subject of the advertisement.

'Just a dream,' Thomas explained.

'Would you rather be your own master than continue in service?' Bellamy asked him.

'Who wouldn't, sir?'

'Any man in his own way of business takes knocks,' Bellamy explained. 'He has to eat a lot of humble pie. Even Members of Parliament. Even the Prime Minister.'

'Begging your pardon, sir,' Thomas replied. 'But servants eat humble pie.'

Seeing that Mr Bellamy was prepared to be cordial and evidently the chosen delegate from upstairs sent to parley with him, Thomas Watkins extended the hand of friendship further with the offer of a glass of beer and a seat.

They discussed the possibilities of life in the garage world as opposed to the world of chauffeuring in some detail.

Then Richard Bellamy made what appeared to be almost a quixotic gesture. He offered the chauffeur the capital sum to buy the garage in Kilburn outright.

At first Thomas protested that it was altogether too generous a gesture and that anyway he was morally engaged to the Chester Square people; little by little he allowed himself to be persuaded round to accepting Mr Bellamy's offer. It was agreed that for the sake of appearances the sudden acquisition of the money should be explained away as a nice windfall from relatives in Wales. In exchange Thomas gave a solemn undertaking that the secrets of the Bellamy household would never be revealed by himself or Sarah.

Mr Bellamy produced his cheque book. Even at this supremely exciting moment Thomas did not lose his sangfroid.

'Pay bearer, if you please, sir,' he said.

That evening there was a celebration in the servants' hall. All past feuds were forgotten in the general alcoholic rejoicing, Mr Hudson proposing a toast to the bride and bridegroom and Mrs Bridges making a sentimental speech about two of her children going out into the great world. Rose had gone out and Ruby remained firmly at her sink taking no part in the proceedings. Mrs Bridges wasn't having her kitchenmaid behaving like that so she sent Daisy to fetch her.

'She's a caution that Sarah,' said Daisy. Sarah got up on a chair in the servants' hall and began giving the company a selection of her old music hall songs. They could see her through the open scullery door.

'She's a caution all right,' Ruby replied, 'having a baby, getting married, coming into all that money.'

Ruby told Daisy that she had overheard Thomas and Sarah quarrelling over the baby months ago. Thomas was the father and the whole story nothing but a pack of lies. Ruby was a simple soul who had been strictly brought up and she was shocked and horrified by Thomas' and Sarah's behaviour.

'But they all think,' said Daisy in amazement, 'Mr Hudson thinks—Upstairs think. Oh, Ruby, what wickedness there is in this world. He's not decent at all. No more decent than anyone! Not if it's his kid all along. Well, fancy.'

'Should we tell?' Ruby asked her.

Daisy shook her head.

'No, it wouldn't do,' she replied. 'You can only tell on people under you, not over you.'

Daisy was young in years but she had already learnt one of the basic rules of survival below stairs.

In the morning room Richard Bellamy poured himself out a stiff whisky and soda and sat down on the sofa next to his wife. Muted sounds of merriment below penetrated the room coming from the direction of the servants' hall.

'Lucky Thomas came in for that windfall,' Richard remarked with some complacence.

Lady Marjorie put down her sewing and smiled at him as she touched his arm.

'It was ridiculously extravagant of you, Richard,' she said, 'but we are well rid of that pair of scallawags.'

CHAPTER THIRTEEN

As Spring came to London in 1910 Elizabeth Kirbridge found to her annoyance that Mrs Descort had been right; unless she gave them extended credit the ladies of Society wouldn't buy her hats. She also found that running a hat shop in Mayfair was a great deal of hard work for very little profit and the novelty of it began to pall on her. At the same time Julius Karekin's interest in Elizabeth gradually lessened. He still came round to the shop in the evening but very often it was to find fault with the unpaid bills and not to ask her to join him for supper. Sometimes she still was asked round to Albany and sometimes she was asked to share his bed but he made it clear to her that she wasn't welcome without an invitation. Elizabeth complained that it was like making an appointment with her dentist; Julius pleaded pressure of work. It annoyed Elizabeth when she found out he was seeing a lot of her father and with his support making good progress up the ladder of Conservative society. It made her feel jealous and excluded.

In April a letter came from James Bellamy, posted when the P & O liner bringing him back from India called at Brindisi.

'"We dock at Tilbury on the fourteenth,"' Lady Marjorie read aloud to her friend Lady Prudence Fairfax.

'That's next week,' Lady Prudence commented.

'"I am bringing,"' Lady Marjorie continued, unable to

keep the surprise out of her voice, '"I am bringing Phyllis Kingman home with me for a few days before she goes to Leamington to stay with her aunt. She's a topping girl, a marvellous horsewoman and a good looker . . ."' Lady Marjorie turned the page anxiously. '"I'm sure you and father will like her. I hope you do because I have already popped the question. Going through the Suez Canal actually . . . so we are sort of . . . engaged."'

The dire word hung in the air and both the ladies looked stunned. No mother likes to be presented with a fait accompli when it comes to her only son's choice of a wife.

'"So looking forward to getting home,"' Lady Marjorie continued reading in a flat voice, '"so on and so forth."' Then she stopped and looked up at Lady Prudence almost in disbelief.

'"P.S.,"' she read, '"I forgot to mention Phyl's pater is a Major in the Army Veterinary Corps. Awfully nice chap and first rate with polo ponies."'

'My dear Marjorie,' Lady Prudence said standing up and touching her friend's hand in sympathy, 'I'd best get home.'

'At least she's not a servant,' Lady Marjorie said with a slightly hysterical laugh. 'Let's hope she's not pregnant.'

'That's hardly likely,' Lady Prudence assured her old friend, 'with her father a vet.'

Downstairs the news of Captain James' imminent arrival and his engagement was greeted with great interest and lively comment.

'If she's a decent girl her father can be a chimney sweep,' said Miss Roberts taking a most unusually liberal view.

'Well that's a good one coming from you, Miss Roberts,' said Rose.

'I gave up hope of Captain James marrying into the aristocracy years ago,' the lady's maid replied.

'You mean after the fun and games he had with S . . .'

'Now let's have a little respect,' Mr Hudson cut in sharply. 'If Captain James has chosen a fiancée she will be entitled to the respect of this household whoever she is.'

He alone had the experience to know that James Bellamy's choice of a wife might greatly affect all their futures.

Lady Marjorie and Richard Bellamy went down in the car to Tilbury to meet James and Miss Kingman. It was a cold, windy day more like February than April. The newspapers were depressing; there was fighting in Albania, great unrest in the cotton trade and the King had a bad attack of bronchitis and was in Biarritz.

Phyllis proved to be a big, handsome girl with lovely auburn hair. On the way back to Eaton Place in the car she hardly drew breath telling them seemingly endless stories of her life in India; by her own admission she had been the most sought after girl in the Club and James clearly thought that he was very lucky to get her. At Eaton Place Phyllis was rather short with Hudson and clapped her hands at Edward telling him quite sharply to mind bumping her small travelling case. During tea she continued her reminiscences of life in the East.

'You see this idiotic fool of a native syce forgot to tighten the girth and they were in full cry after a very fast pig when father's horse stumbled and the saddle slipped.' Phyllis told them, 'Father went under Panther's belly—at full gallop.'

'That sounds most uncomfortable,' said Lady Marjorie, realising a comment was expected.

'Oh it was,' Phyllis agreed. 'He got kicked in the eye and

had to let go; had a cracking fall, broke two ribs and bruised his pelvis. He's entered for the Kadir Cup this year.'

There was a moment of silence while they tried to imagine Major Kingman after a very fast pig.

'I say I'd love another piece of cake,' said Phyllis.

After tea James took her down to the servants' hall. Phyllis made a better first impression downstairs than upstairs.

'Good, strong-looking girl, that's something. Healthy,' said Mrs Bridges, pleased at the justice Miss Kingman had done to her cake.

'Stuck up, I'd say,' said Miss Roberts.

'She'll keep him in order if anyone can,' said Rose.

'I reckon he's scared of her,' said Edward.

'Well what I think is . . .' Ruby began.

'No one wants to know what you think,' Mrs Bridges assured her. 'Now clear the table sharp.'

'Cheer up, Marjorie,' Richard Bellamy said to his wife when they were alone. 'He could have done worse.'

'Oh those dreadful, middle-class army people,' said Lady Marjorie. 'Just because servants and horses are two-a-penny in India they think they're equal to anyone.' By 'anyone' Lady Marjorie meant someone of her own class.

'The backbone of the Empire, my dear,' Richard went on philosophically. 'They sweat it out in places you and I would rather die than live in . . . awful garrisons and camps and bungalows, pestered by flies and snakes and Lord knows what else . . . limp from heat. I think they deserve a bit of comfort if they can get it.'

'I wish the girl wouldn't speak to Hudson as if he was a houseboy,' Lady Marjorie complained.

'That sort of girl learns very quickly,' Richard was determined to look on the bright side. 'Besides, she's nervous; that's why she talks so much drivel.'

Lady Marjorie shrugged her shoulders. 'Am I so frightening?' she asked her husband.

'Not exactly frightening, my dear,' Richard replied trying to put it as nicely as he could. 'Perhaps just a little awe-inspiring—for the daughter of an army vet.'

In Phyllis's favour was the fact that under her influence James looked strong and healthy and had given up drinking heavily and gambling—and he seemed to have completely forgotten about Sarah.

It was unfortunate that the crisis of Elizabeth's affair with Julius Karekin should coincide with her brother's arrival back in England.

A young and very beautiful daughter of a Marquis had come into the shop and chosen two hats and told Mademoiselle to send the account to Mr Julius Karekin at Albany, Piccadilly. It was clumsily done and Karekin was unhappy when Elizabeth told him about it and he apologised to her for hurting her—but he was quite unrepentant. When Elizabeth accused him of using her for one purpose only—to further his career, he replied that he had warned her from the beginning that he was a snob and an adventurer.

'I am dishonest about many things,' he told her, 'but never about love. You are a charming companion, Elizabeth, to lunch and dine and to talk and sleep with. But I am not in love with you.'

'You were always very honest about that,' Elizabeth admitted. 'All along. But you see I didn't believe you. I wanted so much for us to be in love, properly in love.' Julius made a hopeless gesture with his hands.

'I thought you wanted an affair.'

'I dreamed of something more. It was my fault.'

She had found someone mature and intelligent, someone she could look up to and lean on and had made the foolish mistake of falling in love—with an illusion.

'There's very little I can say,' Julius went on. 'Except to beg you not to spoil the happy times we have had together with bitter recriminations. We are both adult people. You are a married woman. Let us preserve for always what was just a charming incident in both our lives.'

Elizabeth nodded her head.

'Yes. I'll try,' she managed to reply.

That evening Elizabeth arrived back at Eaton Place in a mood of black despair. She was tip-toeing past the drawing room hoping to gain her own room without being discovered when she felt the sudden need for a drink. There was brandy on the tray by the door. She opened it gently. The room seemed deserted and she went in. As she shut the door behind her there was a scuffling from the big sofa and James and Miss Kingman emerged from its depths, dishevelled and embarrassed.

It was hardly the happiest circumstance for a reunion between brother and sister.

'Elizabeth, there you are,' said James and went over to kiss her.

'My brave, bronzed brother,' Elizabeth replied, doing her best.

'Oh, this is Phyl . . . er Phyllis Kingman,' James explained. 'Er Phyl . . . my sister Elizabeth.'

'How do you do, Miss Kingman?' Elizabeth didn't move.

'I hear you have a hat shop,' Phyllis said enthusiastically. 'It must be very exciting.'

'I have been managing a hat shop,' Elizabeth replied. 'I am not any more, and it wasn't very exciting.'

There was a damp silence.

'Well anyway you seem to have got hold of a splendid new friend . . . we're so looking forward to meeting him,' said James brightly. Elizabeth burst into tears and rushed out.

'Sorry about that,' James said helplessly. 'She does get upset sometimes.'

'I expect it's because she's very fond of you,' Phyllis replied, 'and perhaps a little jealous. It's very natural especially as her husband didn't come up to scratch. Isn't that what you told me?'

Elizabeth had supper in her room, sending a message down by Rose to say that she was very tired. From that her father guessed that she was in trouble and after dinner he went up to see her.

'How can I just let Julius go out of my life,' she asked, 'when I owe him so much?'

'You owe him nothing, Elizabeth. He bought you and he bought your mother and myself for the price of a hat shop and the lease of this house. He got what he wanted and don't forget it.'

It was just exactly what Elizabeth wanted to hear from someone else except herself.

Richard told her of Julius Karekin's recent successes. He had been asked to become a financial adviser to the Conservative Party, Arthur Balfour had become a close friend and to crown the list of his triumphs he had been elected a member of the Athenaeum Club.

'He has had his pound of flesh,' said Elizabeth.

'If you care to put it that way,' her father agreed. Elizabeth stretched out her arms above her.

'Oh, papa, what is wrong with me?' she asked sadly. 'I do want so much to be married happily and have children . . . just to be ordinary. It seems so easy for other people.' She lowered her arms and sighed. 'Perhaps I never will,' she said.

Richard kissed her gently.

'You will,' he assured her. 'It's just the right man for you hasn't come along yet, that's all, my dear. He will one day. There's plenty of time.'

Richard was right about Phyllis; she improved daily and soon showed herself to be a sensible, pleasant girl with a passion for shopping. Lady Marjorie watched with something like satisfaction as James began to settle back into life in London again and spent more and more time at his club, or his tailor or going down to see his old friends at Windsor and less and less with Phyllis; she knew very well that passionate friendships begun in some lonely Indian garrison town and forced to blossom in the hothouse claustrophobia of a long sea voyage very rarely survived in the cooler, more sophisticated atmosphere of Britain.

May 5th was Lady Marjorie's birthday and by long tradition there was a family celebration upstairs and downstairs at 165 Eaton Place, and this year there was a further cause for joy in the return of the prodigal son. Lady Prudence Fairfax was the only guest from outside the family and when she arrived she told them that the crowds were growing outside Buckingham Palace at the rumour that the King was gravely ill and sinking.

Just before midnight there was a call on the telephone for Richard Bellamy from the Palace. Mr Hudson rang the drawing room extension and couldn't resist putting the instrument to his ear for a moment afterwards. He walked slowly back into the servants' hall.

'Whatever's the matter, Mr Hudson?' Mrs Bridges asked him when she saw his face.

'The King is dead,' he told the servants. 'Let us go quietly to bed.'

In the drawing room they opened the windows and went out onto the balcony. It was a fair, calm night and they could hear Big Ben strike midnight very clearly.

'Freddie Ponsonby told me on the telephone that the Queen herself took Alice Keppel along to his room this afternoon so that she could sit beside him,' said Richard Bellamy.

'Nine years isn't a very long reign,' said Phyllis. Short as was the reign of King Edward the Seventh, there was not a person in that house, hardly a person in the whole country, who did not feel his death as a keen, personal loss.

Lady Marjorie shivered and hunched her shoulders.

'Come inside, Marjorie,' Richard begged her. 'You'll catch cold.'

She shook her head.

'A goose walked over my grave,' she said.

FICTION　　　　　　　　　　　　C69713

Hawkesworth, John.
　　Upstairs, downstairs II; in my lady's
chamber.　[c1972]

　　I. Title.